A Choir of Ill Children

Other books by Tom Piccirilli:

Novels:
Cast in Dark Waters (with Ed Gorman)
Grave Men
A Lower Deep
The Night Class
The Deceased
Hexes
Sorrow's Crown
The Dead Past
Shards
Dark Father

Collections:
Mean Sheep
This Cape is Red Because I've Been Bleeding (Poetry)
A Student of Hell (Poetry)
Deep Into That Darkness Peering
The Dog Syndrome & Other Sick Puppies
Pentacle

Non-fiction:
Welcome to Hell

A Choir of Ill Children

Tom Piccirilli

NIGHT SHADE BOOKS
San Francisco & Portland

First Edition

ISBN
1-892389-58-4 (Hardcover)
1-892389-59-2 (Limited Edition)

Night Shade Books
http://www.nightshadebooks.com

For Michelle, who gives me a reason

I'd like to thank the following people for their friendship,
support and encouragement over the writing of this novel:
Jack Cady, Lee Seymour, Ed Gorman, Bill Pronzini,
Gerard Houarner, Matt Schwartz, Caniglia, T.M. Wright,
Simon Clark, and Tim Lebbon

Extra special thanks to Jeremy Lassen and Jason Williams,
who heard the weird song.

CHAPTER ONE

WE move in spasms.

My brothers because they are conjoined at the frontal lobe, and me—because for me there is no other way to continue moving.

They have three throats and three bodies, three intertwined minds and many feelings, but only one voice. They even have a lover, Dodi Coots, who sleeps at the foot of their king-size bed with the back of her hand brushing Sebastian's ankle. Her breath is tinged with bourbon and chocolate, a few strands of hair wafting against the corners of her mouth.

She does for them now what I always did for them—empties their bedpans, feeds each separate mouth, helps them into their fresh pajamas, gives them sponge baths and assists them in brushing their own teeth, which remain white and perfect from what I can see.

They dream, sweating with their immense brow furrowed, and they tell me their fantasies in whispers. Each mouth forms a different syllable, framing an independent idea, with an individual limit of emotion. Sebastian is full of malice, Jonah with regret, and Cole speaks of love and nothing but love, no matter how hideous his words. They murdered a six-year-old child, or so they said. They're vague about it. On occasion they make it sound like they killed him, and at other times it seems they only discovered him. I can find no body or evidence, no reports of a missing kid, while I listen to their murmured descriptions every night, and still Cole speaks of love.

It's happened before. I once found a dead boy in the swamp.

My brothers face one another with no need to move their lips, conversing inside the single massive bald head and fractured mind. Silently they argue and debate and agree, lying on the bed, nostrils flaring and their hands sometimes flapping. Since birth they've stared into each other's eyes, sharing the same blood flow and coursing neurochemicals. They have only one epiphysis cerebri, also known as the pineal gland, which was called the "third eye" by ancient peoples who believed it to have mystical properties.

This impedes their mammoth brain's capability to produce the hormone melatonin which regulates daily body rhythms, most notably the circadian rhythm of the day/night cycle. Their points of view are skewed by the endless intimacy and proximity. Only inches from one another's noses, breathing the mutually stale air, unable to see much of anything except each other's grimacing faces. As in blind children, they cannot differentiate between morning and midnight.

When they talk to me, they often speak in the first person, and it's sometimes difficult for me to discern who is saying what, and whether they all feel the same way.

Dodi coos in her sleep. She sighs and purrs,

stretching so that her thigh drips moonlight across the floor. Dead leaves brush against the window, tapping softly. She creeps upon my brothers and tastes each of them in turn, stiffly swabbing the bulging curves of their forebrain, sweeping across the trinity of their stunted, twisted bodies. Knuckles brush the head-board, and four sets of feet whirl and kick.

I force myself not to look and end up staring at the wall instead. As the moon descends it draws their writhing shadows into focus, and I see the amazing things she does with every pliable cusp and muscle as they utter her name with flicking tongues. A name full of bitterness, reluctance, and wonder.

Her mother, Velma Coots, gave Dodi to me in trade for digging some screw worms out of her two cows and fixing the roof of her shanty. The years of humidity and rain and Spanish moss bleeding into the wood had rotted it to tissue. My brothers and I are the richest men in the town of Kingdom Come, Potts County, and still the conjure woman found it necessary to pay me. The price didn't matter to her, I knew. Only the service and finality of exchange.

Dodi got into my truck holding a small bundle of dirty clothes in her lap and didn't say a word. I wasn't even sure she could speak until she woke me one night, between all of their legs, caged by their bones, hidden under all that flesh, and whimpering, "*Jesus, help me now and at the hour of my death, you bastard.*"

It's not something you want to hear. Other men might have argued or refused Velma Coots, which is why she did not trade Dodi to anyone but me, and why I didn't dig screw worms out of anybody else's cows but hers. The conjure woman stood in her yard beside water elm and loblolly pine, with her chin jutting, waiting to see what might happen next.

I waited too. My father killed himself because he could not accept backwoods swamp water ways like this, even though he'd never left Potts County himself. He fought the tradition of his own past and paid his price for it.

I shook my head and drove off with Dodi. No matter what I had to do, I would not end up like my father.

WE may have a sister too, but I can't be certain. Our parents never said anything to me about it, but there are odd indentations along the left side of my rib cage, pointed and with attitude, which could be a woman's features.

Or they could be bruises and welts that never faded from some childhood scuffle. Or knife scars from the drunken brawls in the back of barrooms. Or perhaps fingernail scratches from one of the roadhouse gals I can't remember. They are beautiful and unforgettable when the icy beer and triple boilermakers wear down the spiked edges of the world enough to become bearable for another minute. The middle-aged women slow dance with me across the wet floor of Leadbetter's, denying their anguish as we move, in spasms, out to the parking lot and into the back of my truck.

JONAH has fallen in love with Sarah, who is doing a student documentary about my family.

She's been staying in the house a couple of weeks now, along with her cameraman, Fred. She tries to interview me but thinks I'm only another witless Kingdom Come swamp rat losing my mind to one-sixty proof moonshine. She's got the high lilt of a Jewish American Princess straight from the Gold Coast of Long Island, but she enjoys passing herself off as an East Village bohemian.

There's a tattoo on her hip that peeks out whenever she stands on her toes to fix the cheap halogen lights and the aluminum parabolic reflectors, but I can't make out what it might be. It's not sharp work and the colors already appear faded. Her navel is pierced, which I find sort of sexy. There's a slight scar around the piercing from where infection had set in. She's the kind of girl who might smuggle hashish in the binding of D.M. Thomas' *The White Hotel*. Sarah wants to be eccentric but just doesn't have the stomach for it.

Being around my brothers terrifies her, and she can't hold back her staggering nausea. Sebastian chuckles as she grows pale talking with them, doing her best not to gag but still turning a nice shade of green, swallowing down her bile. She talks about the Sundance Film Festival, repeating the words like a mantra.

Sebastian says those words too, all of their tongues flailing. My brothers speak as one, each mouth working like a pipe organ, playing a different portion of their communal speech. It's the way that brain works. The "ch" goes to Sebastian, along with the glottal noises, "uh" and "ooh," "ing," names of foreign countries and pronouns, anything that brings his teeth together.

Jonah gets the hisses, the "ph" and drawn out orgasmic "eeeeeee," titles of symphonies and sit-coms, all the poetry.

Cole is left with the growls and hard consonants,

the adverbs, numbers following ten, dirty words, colors, sweet nothings, and every predicate.

Trying to hold back her fear, Sarah does a fair amount of cocaine and leaves blood-spotted tissues in the waste basket and sitting on the rim of the toilet seat. She has to be careful when she reaches into her handbag so that she doesn't cut her fingers on the razor blades. Every so often she gives such an implosive sniff that there's a loud, high-pitched whistle. She left her nose on some Manhattan surgeon's floor and didn't quite get what her father paid for.

Fred sets up the camera and plays with his light meter, taking readings all over the living room. He uses a Tiffen Black Pro Mist Filter No. 1/2 to knock the bite off glass, wet teeth, brass, and the harshness of my brothers' appearance. I watch him with a slight smile which he gives in return, rolling his eyes as he spins away towards the bay window, playing with the blinds. He says, "Fuckin' freak shitkickers" loud enough for me to hear because he thinks I'm too stupid to consider it an insult.

I don't take offense, really, but it sets a smoldering fire in my guts, and I'm going to break his arm in two places anyway.

Jonah, who is remorseful, scowls and holds his lips apart, filling each syllable he gets to say with all his resentment. He forces Sebastian and Cole to wheel farther and farther around as they walk so he can get as close to Sarah as possible. He's making a hell of an effort. You can hear their joints popping, the odd slap of nearly atrophied muscle on muscle. Their legs are like contorted stems bending beneath their combined weight. Arms twine around each other's waists like they're about to break out into a bizarre Russian dance.

Jonah rubs against Sarah like an animal, which is exactly how she thinks of him and the others and me. She chokes back puke. We are generally beneath notice, but not beneath disgust, and when she finally gets what she wants down on film she'll wish us dead in the river.

I sit on the settee and try to look stupid without drooling. It's easier than it should be. She has a DAT recorder thrust into the middle of the room and a mini-cassette recorder on the table placed precisely equidistant from us both. She asks the same questions repeatedly, hoping to keep me talking long enough so that even if I don't give an adequate answer, I'll say enough for her to splice the tape together into something worthwhile.

"Tell me, Thomas, what is it like living with a Siamese triplet?"

There is no such thing, of course—the term is a misnomer as she uses it, proving how ignorant she is of the situation. But I can't completely fault her for that. There's no way to comprehend it, even for us. "Oh, it's fine."

"Could you elucidate?"

I lean forward towards the recorder. "It's fine!"

Her grin is soldered in place, and her upper row of crowns look like they might snap to pieces at any moment. Her nose hairs are being burned away by the coke. "No, Thomas," she says through her teeth. "Elucidate doesn't mean louder, it means could you go into a little more depth about that?"

"About what?"

"Living with your brothers."

I lean forward. "We get along just fine!"

The mini-tape recorder makes a soft whirr as she

swallows thickly. The pulse under her left ear throbs so wildly that it brushes her long gold earrings and gets them swinging. I must admit that Sarah is quite an attractive girl, and I realize why Jonah is falling in love with her despite her poor disposition. What I don't understand is why Sebastian and Cole aren't.

It's a good thing Fred is using the Mist Filter because Sarah's tongue unfurls and is very slimy. "Why do you sleep in the same bedroom?"

"It's my room."

"You have a gorgeous antediluvian mansion here that's enormous enough to fit five families under one roof."

I nod and tell her, "It's nice."

"Don't you need privacy? Why do you sleep in the same bedroom as your brothers?"

"I always have. It's our room. We watch over one another." Which is nothing less than the truth.

The edges of her nostrils are threaded with broken blood vessels, a sharp pink that is both revolting and somehow arousing. Her hair is plum-colored, breasts slightly too large just the way Jonah likes them. Perfect caps that are not too white or too large, and the tip of her tongue constantly works across the glossy upper lip. Her insincerity bleeds off her in a torrent now. Jonah's using his peripheral vision to stare at Sarah and somehow let his love be known. He's beginning to jitter and giggle in place, which means all three of them are. The pleasure in his mind is a delight for them all.

Fred tries to hold his rancor and derision in but can't make it. I see him coming apart inch by inch as the veins stand out in his muscular throat. He lets loose a bark of loathing and aims the camera at the window, searching for Dodi who's swinging from an old tire out front. He zooms in on her, trying to get beaver shots. "Sarah, I'm sick of this place and these freaks. Let's just get out of here and do the movie about your grandmother's Alzheimer's."

"No."

"It can't be any less engaging than this. Come on, an old lady dressed in pig-tails and diaper, calling for her Mommy? That's priceless material."

"The story's here."

"The retards are here, and we've got nothing to show for our time so far except a huge credit card bill. That car rental is costing us and I've got to get the DAT back to the university by next Wednesday or Professor James is gonna throw a fit. I signed for this hardware, I'm responsible for it."

She tries to hold on, pressing her nails on top of the cassette recorder and shoving it closer to me. "Yours is one of the richest and oldest families in the town of Kingdom Come, but you seem to be ostracized by the community."

"They bring us pies sometimes."

"Pies?"

"Sour Cream Rhubarb, Mississippi Mud, Tar Heel Pie." Some folks do bring us homemade meals on occasion, but usually it's me doing the baking and giving food away to the men at the mill.

Though Jonah is irritated, Sebastian likes the way I'm screwing with her. He shouts out the names of more pies, using all their throats: Peach Skillet, Double Layer Pumpkin, Sweet Potato, Kiwi Lime.

Sarah's eyes are almost spinning. The coke is really grooving in her system. She can't focus well and I'm breaking down what little concentration she has left. If only she'd listened to me that first day when I told her we weren't interested in broadcasting our lives. She'd been in control then, so wonderfully sure of herself. Backing off the porch she had turned her attention to my brothers, who peered through the bay window and rapped on the glass with their many hands. Jonah, all three of them actually, begging Sarah to stay.

She's spoken with them at length but still needs me for the buffer. The tale cannot work without my support. The audience needs someone to identity with. This is, after all, a human interest story.

MAGGIE stands on the back lawn staring up at our bedroom window.

The house is large and accommodating, with three floors, six bedrooms, and a century and a half of ghosts packed within its walls. Rich divans, exquisitely carved furniture, velvet draperies, and magnificent mantelpieces adorn almost every room.

Generations of our family have lived and weakened here. Our name is revered and cursed, as it probably should be. That's all right. The grudge of money and the unyielding myth of the wealthy go hand in hand. An ancestor founded the town. Our great-grandfather built the mill. Our father leaped into its furious machinery one rainy summer night. And our mother vanished just days before his suicide.

Legend and language form their own religion here in Kingdom Come, Potts County.

When I was nine, a black boy from up the road, Drabs Bibbler, a preacher's son who'd been touched by the bitter spirit of God, married me and Maggie down by the river's edge.

He baptized us and gave witness and sang hymns too, showing us how to rejoice and dance in praise of the Lord. Before the day was out he fell to thrashing in a fit of tongues and shrieked out his despair. She and I watched on the shore as Drabs slid down the muddy bank on his back, wailing in an unknown language and heaving until he was out of sight.

No matter what anybody told us after that, Maggie and I knew we were man and wife from that day forward, though we never so much as shared a kiss.

She stares up at me now with all the passion, affection and devotion the human heart can muster, and soon she begins to weave in the wind. Her white dress whirls like an unwrapped shroud until she eventually becomes just another part of the dark and endless night.

DRABS Bibbler is walking down the road naked when I pull over and offer him a lift. He gets into the truck and doesn't say anything for about five miles. Finally, he looks over and I can see that he's welling up. The teardrops are spilling down his face across the burn scars on his neck and chest. He's been in love with Maggie since long before the day he wed her to me, but he can't tear asunder what he helped God to unite. It's killing him and has been for twenty years. Maybe it's killing all of us.

"The hell are you doing?" I say.

"You're going to ask me that?"

It was a stupid question. When he's in this state I can't talk to him. No one can. I do my best to make sure he survives his own sorrow. If another white woman spots his flopping pecker swaying in the breeze the rednecks aren't going to be happy with beating the hell out of him and swabbing his body with hot tar. They're going to lynch and castrate him for sure.

I wonder if he'll fall into tongues again, which almost always happens when I'm in his presence for more than twenty minutes.

"I'm going to give up the church," he tells me. "My daddy's church, really. I was never any good at it to begin with and I get worse with each passing week. The congregation hates me."

"No they don't, they just get scared. They don't know any better."

"My daddy don't want me up on his pulpit."

It's true. Reverend Bibbler preaches about Paradise but his own son frightens the parishioners off. "What are you planning to do instead?"

"I'm not certain yet."

"Maybe you should keep on preaching until you figure it out."

"No, I want it to end," Drabs says with a sneer. "I feel like a fraud and a damn fool up there."

He can still make me chuckle at the most inopportune times. "At least you wear clothes at the altar."

"That's true, I do. But I'm still only lying."

"You've got enough of God in your life already. Do something else that you might enjoy."

"There isn't anything."

His commitment to Maggie is so intense that it envelops him like the crimson nimbus of a burning flare. It isn't a pure love but it'll do until one comes along. He's had many women in Potts County and fathered a half dozen children I know about. He takes no responsibility for anyone or anything except my baptism and marriage. Nothing else makes any real impression on him.

"I've been having visions about you," Drabs says.

"You've always had visions about me."

"More now than ever," he says, and the sorrow is so great in his voice that I want to leap out of the truck.

"Anything interesting?"

The angles of his shining handsome black face fall in on themselves as he frowns. "I keep seeing a Ferris Wheel. It's damn small. And a merry-go-round. The horses' faces are all chipped."

My life, going up and down, around and around, broken. "That's not the Holy Spirit, that's Freud."

"And another thing…there's a man who's biting the head off a live snake, covered in chicken parts."

"A geek," I say. "Jesus Christ, Drabs, don't tell me you see me winding up as a geek."

"No, no, listen. It's not you, but he's willing to talk to you, for the price of a pint of moonshine."

"Six bits. Do I give it to him?"

His fingers carelessly brush his chest scars as he nods, staring off through the windshield at the tree line. "Yes."

I feel the slow drifting chill begin to prickle my scalp. I know better than to ignore Drabs now. "What's he saying?"

Drabs turns in his seat with his mouth open but the tongues are abruptly upon him. Maybe I've brought this on us, simply by asking. Whatever he wants to tell me is important to him, and he tries to fight. Sweat streams across his face and his fingers twitch like a handful of wasps. I grab the steering wheel tighter and whisper, "Leave him alone, damn you."

Entreaties don't matter much in the presence of the Lord. There is no petition, and I've always known it. Drabs hurls himself hard against the passenger door, the spirit bearing down on him, as he yells in a language I feel I could almost understand if only he'd slow down a little.

I pull up to his long dirt driveway and wheel around towards the back. I get out and ease him into a wet patch of yard so he won't hurt himself. The chickasaw plum and sparkleberries sway against my shoulders. The words rush from him furiously until he's foaming at the mouth, choking on them.

The muscles of his face are being yanked in directions they shouldn't go. He tumbles and bounces viciously, flails sideways underneath a willow tree, and rolls through the brush until he's eventually lost behind the glowing green cypress.

I smoke half a pack of cigarettes waiting to see if he'll come back, but he never does.

CHAPTER TWO

IN the deepest hour of the night, my mother used to dream of Cole unfolded from Sebastian and Jonah, arising in the moonlight to stand complete and alone. They smile at each other and hug, and I wind up with pangs of spite making me grit my teeth.

It's a dream that has somehow been passed on from her to me. Cole speaks in a singular forgiving voice, full of love, saying my name as though there is an extra meaning there that I don't yet realize.

But I'm not falling for it. We have expectations and are prepared to do what we must to meet them. The dream is destined to become nightmare, of course. Mama turns and her mouth is red, the blood leaking out onto the floor. She needs help but she doesn't want it, and I can't get anywhere near her. She spins aside and is lost in the shadows. When Cole speaks my name from the doorway he is glancing down at the bed where I have replaced him among the others.

I can barely flap my dwarfed and bent arms, these diminutive bony legs wreathed around theirs. Our kneecaps clatter together. I can't see anything but the glaring eyes of Sebastian and Jonah, who hate the way that I hate, and who do horrible things to me inside our shared ten-pound brain.

ONE of the road house girls from Leadbetter's shows up at the house to tell me she's pregnant.

I don't remember her face at all, not even when she moves, in spasms, to kiss me like we're long-time lovers.

But when she sits in the love-seat on the porch alongside me, subtly shifting her weight to show the inseam of her thigh, a suddenly clear and painful memory hits. She is Betty Lynn, and she's barely nineteen.

Her youth hangs off her like baby fat. She thinks she's sly and now she'll have something to tell the other kids down at the Piggly Wiggly and Doover's Five & Dime. It looks like her mother did her makeup and hair this afternoon. She went light on the eyeshadow, heavy on the rouge. Her flowered print summer dress has been freshly pressed and she smells faintly of an old lady's dull perfume.

I can just see her mama giving her pointers on what to say and do now. Don't scare him off, don't be threatenin'. Reel him in slow like a catfish and don't jerk the line. This is gonna be her one big break in life, Mama talking with hairpins jutting from between her teeth, telling Betty Lynn how to act in order to get a man, combing out her knotted curls. This is a chance for money and family. To get out of the river bottoms and live in a mansion. For something different to happen in a town where nothing ever changes except the extent of desperation.

Betty Lynn has never seen a home as huge as ours,

and immediately she begins to imagine herself living here without her five screaming younger brothers and sisters always pinching at her legs. No chickens to feed and kill and pluck, no cows to milk, no tarpaper shack that collects heat in the summer and pours it over you like scalding water. She grins and shows off her tiny square teeth, eyes wide and starry, thinking about what she'll buy first once she gets her fists on some cash. That's natural enough, everyone in Potts County does the same thing.

She takes in the empty space and wonderful silence for a minute, picturing the size of the closets and the depth of the bathtubs. All this room, it's got to be put to use. She knows she's going to be mother to a screaming brood, that's her fate no matter what else happens to her, but it would be so much more endurable if she could wear lavish pleated dresses and drink Chablis. If she could finally afford disposable diapers and not have to washboard the cloth ones anymore. Mama is slowly suffocating her, the kids around her knees are crushing her, the chickens clucking in the kitchen driving her crazy, oh hell yes, everything is.

Her pale blue eyes are swirling as the smile begins to creep from the corners of her mouth and broadens further. She cannot pronounce Chablis and has never tasted it, but she'll learn to drink it. Nothing's worse than Daddy's mash whiskey, and he's only got half a tongue left now because of it. Betty Lynn wants to be valued by those in high society, however they act. Wherever they are and whatever they do. *That's* how it's going to be, Mama said. And *that's* exactly what she wants to tell them down at the Piggly Wiggly and Doover's Five & Dime when they back up and turn away in awful seething jealousy.

She speaks her mind, which is how it should be. "I think we ought to get married."

"You do."

"Uh huh. I'd make a good wife and a fine mother. I've pretty much had to raise my brothers and sisters since Papa got too sick to work anymore. I handle them all right, and I'll handle this child just the same."

"You seem to know what you want," I say.

"You did too, that night in the parking lot."

"Yes," I admit. It's true enough, or at least had been at the time. I used a condom though but I don't bother to press the point. Nothing I say to her is going to amount to anything much. I get off the loveseat and offer her my hand. "Come on, let's go inside."

"You want me to go inside with you?"

"Sure."

Perhaps she's heard the rumors about my brothers but she can't possibly believe they're true. It's a tale meant only to scare local kids. Something to be discarded alongside the bogeyman and the flat rock ghosts. Her eyes are bright as she glances at the mantel and the carved furniture. Fred and Sarah have taken Dodi with them to Leadbetter's, and the house is silent and feels as if it hasn't been lived in for fifty years. We walk past the stairway and the steps draw our attention like a siphon. The darkness pools.

"What's up there?"

"My brothers."

That gets a nervous chuckle from her as she toes the floor. She touches her fancy hairdo to make sure it hasn't started to unravel yet. "Naaaw."

"Yes."

"Aw, you're just fooling me."

"No, it's true."

She presses a finger to my chest, so shy here in this maze of hallways. My wrist flicks against the underside of her right breast and her perfume doesn't smell so bad anymore. She looks up and down the stairs, smiling but drawing away, expecting some fun surprises. "I don't think I believe you."

"Come see for yourself."

We head up the steps hand in hand. We're going to visit the Easter Bunny and Santa Claus. She can hardly contain herself and lets loose with a few giggles. It's a sweet sound. We're going to make love for hours on a grand bed, and then I'll present her with my grandmother's three carat diamond ring. Or maybe Betty Lynn thinks I'm taking her to the master bedroom to show her all the excessive closet space. To lay her down on silk sheets, dapple her pale cheeks with rose petals, and read *Les Fleurs Du Mal* to her in French. I've done it to others.

I pause at the bedroom door and let the moment extend. I'm giggling a little too, and that startles me. She steps closer as if I might lift her into my arms and carry her across the threshold. I open the door and take her by the hand, leading her into the gray shadows to the bodies on the bed.

For a second you might think there are parts of corpses stacked up on the mattress, pieced together, still quivering.

"I'm getting married!" I tell my brothers.

They struggle off the bed, thrusting the tremendous conjoined head forward first, followed by the three trunks and a circle of stunted tangled limbs.

"Oh my sweet Jesus," Betty Lynn whispers in a

feeble voice, "save my soul. Mama, mama, you never told me—"

Sebastian, who despises and detests, uses all three of their mouths to softly spew his venom. "Get out of here, you useless stupid cunt."

They begin laughing weakly, and hearing that fluted sound is like listening to a choir of ill children.

I reach for my wallet and grab enough cash to cover the abortion. I hold a handful of bills out to her but she rushes past without taking any.

The faint rippling laughter follows Betty Lynn's scuttling and cries as she clambers down two flights of stairs, tripping and tumbling. Awful moans dredge up from deep inside her. She's bitten through her tongue and droplets of blood spatter the steps. She beats at her somewhat flabby belly, hoping to kill the creature inside her before it can grow into *that*.

Before it can become me.

BY the time they get back, Fred has pretty much scrapped the idea of making a documentary and now wants to film a porno movie starring Dodi Coots and Drabs Bibbler. He hasn't met Drabs yet but he must've seen him naked and sobbing on the back roads with his pecker flouncing in the breeze. I hate to admit it, but the flick would probably go over well on the amateur video market.

"How much money we talking about here?" Dodi asks him. She catches my eye as if she's just kidding around but I'm sure she toys with the idea.

"Depends on the number and variety of scenes we get."

Fred, who's always thinking, has to keep his target

audience in mind. The kink market isn't as large or prevalent as the main porno scene out of Van Nuys, but they're willing to pay a lot more for something genuinely original. If he could get his camera into our bedroom, set the lights up right without any filter this time, and find the proper angles—

"Can they ejaculate?" he asks.

"Who?" Dodi asks.

"Who do you think? The triplets. Can they ejaculate?"

"The hell kind of question is that?"

"An honest one," he says. "They share the same forehead, for Christ's sake. I was curious, that's all."

"Yes, they can. Now you've got your answer."

"Good. Then we can get the money shot. Three of them, in fact. Can you handle that?"

It doesn't bother him talking in front of me, treating me like this in my own house. He's leering so widely that I can see his rotted back teeth, the partial upper bridge that isn't quite making it.

The stink of rum wafts by. Sarah is drunk, and it's not mixing well with the cocaine. She's frowning so hard that you could stick a ten-penny nail in the wrinkle between her eyes and it wouldn't fall out. She's muttering names loudly and spitting like a cat.

Fred is filled with the idea of his new destiny as an independent porno maker: you've got freaks, gang bang, underage Dog Patch vixen, just put her in pigtails, and each new element of kink drives up the going price. What else can he add? He looks around the room and takes a couple of hesitant steps towards the fireplace. Torture with the poker? Branding? He eyes Sarah. She's wasted enough not to notice if he urges her into a dark room to bed a mutant.

He sits and cuts his stash and does a few lines of coke off a hand-held mirror, offering the rest to the girls. They each snort enough to ice their higher brain functions nicely. It surprises me that Dodi would try it. She begins to chuckle at the dust motes falling in sunbeams. Her mother's swamp spells never prepared her for this and a sob breaks inside her chest. A deep red flush washes across her chest and up to her neck as she draws nearer to Sarah. I'm aroused but I also find myself rankled and feeling wedged into a violent corner.

Dodi's in the mood and I have a voyeuristic streak. I watch, still giving my dim vague smile as she reaches over and grasps Sarah's chin with both hands, pointing their lips towards each other. Fred starts playing with his cameras and tapes. Dodi is barely five feet tall and weighs ninety pounds, but she's pure muscle. Sarah struggles a little but not much as Dodi drops forward and forces an open-mouth kiss. One of them lets loose a soft growl. Or maybe it's me. For some reason I keep thinking this is going to end in murder.

They work into it slowly, Sarah making small whines and trying to push Dodi off, both her hands on Dodi's breasts. Shove, shove, and then she begins to squeeze gently. It's the thing of male fantasies. Dodi coos and hums, the same as she does when she's snaking among my brothers. She gives a sidelong glance to see who's watching. I am. Fred, though, is thinking only of freaks, and suddenly makes a bee-line towards the stairway.

I sigh because this good thing is over even before I get to see either of the girls naked. Fred is fast and light on his feet, but I beat him to the corridor and block the way. He's so used to looking through me that he seems unsure as to why he can't make it to the stairs. His head tilts to one side. He's puzzled, wondering what's stopping him. He can't figure out what the problem is.

I have to clear my throat a few times before Fred finally focuses in. He's got me by twenty-five pounds and three inches, and puts a heavy palm on my chest to nudge me aside. He looks confused when I don't fall over. Fred exerts more pressure and still nothing happens. He makes a noise like an infant trapped in a playpen who wants to get out.

"Move it!" he shouts. "You stupid bastard! I'm on a mission, this is a lifework now. Get out of the way!"

His vehemence makes me think I'm wrong about the way this is going. Maybe he's the one who really wants to get it on with my brothers. An extra kink, go for the gay gang bang mutant market.

It's a little surprising that the situation has arrived at critical mass so soon. Things must be resolved quickly, cleanly, and efficiently. If I simply throw Fred out then Sarah will leave too, and Jonah will be inconsolable. It's going to happen eventually but I'd rather put it off for as long as I can.

Jonah's up there already beginning to squawk and croon, the poetry pouring into the air. *"For where she lies, my swept drifted spirit follows, the course unmatched and not known, nor cared for, whether it dies or is kept..."*

Fred grabs me by the throat and starts tightening his grip. "You retarded banjo-playing backwoods son of a bitch! Didn't you hear me? I said get the fuck out of my way!"

I try finding a place where I can strike without doing any real internal damage to him, but he's got my blood up. Maybe it was the banjo line. I've always wanted to learn how to play. His fists tighten even more and he's trembling in his fury, his bad upper bridge squeaking against his splintered teeth as he snarls and squeals.

I follow my course. I let go with two taps to his solar plexus and he immediately crumples at the foot of the stairs. If I brought my fists down on the sweet spot of his skull it would shatter like ancient pottery.

Instead, I grab him by the hair and drag him into the kitchen. Fred puffs his cheeks up with air and lets his breath out in one long streaming hiss. He's trying to shake it off and those fists flash out again. He's had enough coke to wire a rhino so this has to be done carefully. It shouldn't take much scotch to get him under, but the question is how much can he swallow before his heart gives out.

I pour about a quarter pint down his gullet before he lets out a twittering burp and his eyes roll up into the back of his head. Every muscle in his body liquefies at once and he slowly crimps and spreads across the floor.

Dodi and Sarah have left the living room and are nowhere in the house. My truck is gone.

"...unmatched and not known, nor cared for, whether it dies..."

SOMEBODY has been kicking dogs in town.

Children cry in the streets hysterically calling their pets' names while parents glower at every neighbor. The dogs are angry and won't accept offered treats. The boot size appears to be a twelve, just a little larger than my own. The dogs have grown cautious and suspicious, slinking around the yards and hiding behind the water elm and white oak.

Even the conjure women and granny-witches who live

in the bottoms don't know what to do about it. They weave their charms and wipe various concoctions all over the hounds, meant to drive away the mischief. Now the dogs aren't only angry but they smell awful too. Their fur is slicked back and gummed up, streaked with foul grease and colorful powders. Some of the children are allergic to the potions. Terrible hives as fat as tubers rise on moppet faces.

The townsfolk have grown paranoid, searching out size twelve boots. If you wear an eleven and a half or a twelve and a half, you still get frightful glances and scowls. Percy's Ammo and Tackle Shop has had a run on shotgun shells. The granny witches empty the swamp of frogs, newts, bats, and nightcrawlers.

Red clouds and vicious stenches rise from their smoke-stacks, fumes swirling above Kingdom Come. Velma Coots lops off a pinkie in sacrifice. The price doesn't matter to her. Only the service and finality of exchange.

I'm beginning to suspect that lady's sanity.

Eyeless newts and legless toads are tossed out shack windows and thrown back into the bayou. Heaps of them lay struggling and dying in the morass, crawling and cling-ing together. The dogs are too angry to play with any-more, and the children have taken to carrying crippled frogs, blind newts and wingless bats around—naming them, trading them, affixing tiny collars and leashes, sun-glasses and carts.

The elixirs continue to boil but the dogs aren't pro-tected.

None of us are.

MY father knew evil. It came for him in the shape of his own past.

From birth he was as rooted to Potts County, the mill and his family name as I am rooted to my brothers and they are rooted to one another. Evil, as considered in these cases, is a lack of choice.

He had a destiny confined to the town, but he was never afforded much vision or imagination. He was a realist with too much fervor and not enough reverie. He always remained pragmatic in a place that had too much use for superstition. That's enough to ruin any man.

But he did his best, or what he considered to be his best, most of the time. He used his wealth in an attempt to better the lives of the citizens of Kingdom Come even when they didn't want what he had to contribute. He built schools and homes and even a hospital. He attempted to drain the swamp in order to let a highway pass by that would allow these people alternatives.

My father had been a practical man but hardly a sensible one. The schools sat empty until the storm and wind damage wore them away inch by inch. You couldn't blame the people of Potts County just because the board of education hadn't offered any kind of a useful curriculum. Chemistry in a tube wasn't pertinent. The wheel of the universe didn't turn when the cream went bad. Logarithms, geometry, and algebra did not apply to the height of the river during flood season.

And who exactly could afford the time for that sort of schooling? Crops needed planting, fence posts fixed, grandpa's colostomy bag cleaned out, and rituals to be performed. The new houses became hovels filled with pigs, goats, and buckets of slop. There are men who do not yet trust light bulbs.

The vacant hospital that bore my father's name couldn't run without the sick and eventually closed its doors. Kingdom Come had found its medicine in the granny witches and bog bottoms for a hundred years, and the doctors wouldn't take eggs or turpentine in trade.

Draining the swamp was impossible and everybody knew it. Even my Dad knew it, I think. It was an act of arrogance and pride on his part, and he deserved whatever happened because of his conceit. Despite an army of screaming machinery and a parade of two hundred men, he never cleared a whole foot of the bayou. Each failure brought him closer to the living heart of his own hatred.

My father loved my brothers better than me, which I can understand and even respect. He cared for them in the same way a hostage learns to show regard for his captor, as the tortured comes to welcome the rope, and a suicide grows eager for the skinning knife of his own flaying. This is a rare and ultimate grace.

He had no other choice, which means that his love, too, added to the killing of him.

Evil followed my father through every minute of his life, including the final instant when he threw himself into the mill. Palpable, omnipresent, and altogether indifferent. It's an anguish I've come to understand over the years. I fill his clothes and shoes. We are nearly the same size and take up almost an equal amount of displacement in the world. We are virtually the same height and weight, with the identical name. His void lives on, awaiting me in this house, beyond the weeds, at the center of the shower, and breathing heavily in back of my truck.

I am as grounded to my brothers as if I were one

of them. Which I am.

So I continue checking the paper for a missing six-year-old kid or some word on my mother, and still there's no mention of either.

ABBOTT Earl is a hell of a square dancer even in his robes. He hikes them up and shows off his salt-stump knees to everyone at the barn dance. There are trails and spatters of blood across his skin because he's a penitent who's sewn catclaw briars and thorns into his vestments. He calls out with an occasional "Yee Ha!" which he doesn't consider to be talking. He can only speak at sixth hour, according to his vows.

I keep waiting for Drabs to show up but he doesn't. I look out the windows at the dogs cowering in the dirty straw. Maggie stands on the other side of the barnyard, wary, gliding easily away from me whenever I move towards her.

We circle like angry, heated beasts.

THEY hold a town meeting to find out what to do about the dogs being kicked, but folks are so scared to leave Spot and Cody and Byron and Sienna and Criswell and all the others behind for the evening that only a few people show up. Cat lovers mostly, I suspect.

Sheriff Burke is having a hard go of it, pawing his chin. "At this time, we have no suspects."

"No suspects, you say!" shouts Velma Coots, who has given a pinkie hoping to get to the bottom of this, and she expects no less sacrifice from the police. "I believe that every man wearing size twelve shoes is a suspect, for sure! That's how it seems to me. And don't you turn a blind eye to any woman with big feet either."

There is hesitant agreement and some nods of approval from all around the room.

Burke is a little man who suffers from short guy syndrome. He's piqued and always keeps his hat and boots on to gain the extra few inches. His insecurities show through every time he tries to drop his squeaky voice by an octave. Sometimes he's too excited and forgets to talk from his diaphragm, and this reedy piping escapes him. He waves his arms around like a drowning child, the fury filling his face. "That's true, Velma, and we've been through the local footwear shops already in order to obtain shoe-size records. While we've questioned several men and women, at this time we have no single chief suspect."

Velma Coots glares at Burke's pinkies with so much animosity that he's nearly brushed over by her vitriol. He makes tiny fists.

"So what are people to do?" asks Drabs' father, Reverend Clem Bibbler. No matter how badly it breaks a hundred degrees I've never seen him sweat. He's taking this situation extremely seriously, but as quietly and calmly as possible. Members of his congregation have stopped attending services because they're afraid to leave their dogs and hive-riddled children home alone. And also because they're frightened that Drabs might start taking his clothes off at the altar.

"Everyone's being asked to take certain precautions," Burke tells the reverend. "Don't leave your loved ones out at night. Bring them inside. Keep as good a watch over them as you do your own children. Don't let them alone over long periods. Make sure your gates are locked. Undo the chains. Keep your guns loaded and close to you at all times. Keep a round in the chamber. If you must leave your home for an extended amount of time, hire a sitter. I've also been authorized to employ three new part-time deputies who are currently assisting me on this case."

Prayers aren't helping. Perhaps Reverend Bibbler has put too much pressure on God lately, diverting His divine attention and diluting the Lord's power.

For twenty years he's been begging the Almighty to bring his boy Drabs back to his senses, and now all of a sudden he expects miracles over a few booted poodles. Even he cannot fathom the full extent of his folly, and he's obviously ashamed just in the asking. The more I think about it the more I realize how incongruous Reverend Bibbler has become in Potts County. I'd pity the man if I wasn't so sure that, like my father, he's brought this on himself.

"We want justice!" someone cries.

"Blood!"

"We don't want our kids playing with legless frogs anymore!"

"Or crippled bats!"

"We're going to catch this clever kicker," the sheriff tells them. He finds me in the audience and scowls in my direction. When it all comes down to it, he harbors a grudge against my family for having settled the county. All troubles track back to us.

Burke is as small as a white lie and looks as if he might be carried off under the arm of a hefty woman at any second. He feels it too, and smiles cruelly.

THE Holy Order of Flying Walendas.

They like the metaphor of walking the high wire through life, putting your faith in God and in your own responsible preparation. I still think there must be some kind of legal infringement here, but every year it seems that there are more monks and less Walendas.

Abbott Earl drove one of the bulldozers my father hired to drain the swamp. He was good at his job, as were all the workers, but they still couldn't accomplish the task set before them. When my father died, he took something from those loyal men who had vainly fought alongside him. Abbott Earl lost his way for a time and continued to stay in town, living at the bottom of a tequila bottle and bedding a one-eyed woman named Lucretia Murteen.

He found his faith again when he awoke covered in vomit and blood lying on the icy floor of the vacant hospital. The front windows had been shattered long ago but he'd still somehow sliced open his forearm climbing inside. Perhaps he'd been attempting to kill himself. There were three deep vertical gashes from his wrist to halfway up his arm. If he'd meant to do it then he'd been earnest about dying at the time.

God was there with him, he said, and I have no reason to disbelieve him. The hospital was completely empty except for one pack of bandages, which was just enough for him to tie off his flowing wounds. That kind of coincidence would have made me think twice too. I sold the place to him for a dollar, which he immediately converted into a monastery.

Spiritual seekers from all over the world have made their pilgrimages to Kingdom Come and settled into the order. Their races, religions, and shades of their features are as varied as any in the world. Some are prophets, or might be. Others are acolytes hoping to pierce dimensions and stand between the pillars of heaven. Some are alcoholics and drug addicts looking for a last chance at redemption.

In meditation anything is allowed. They sweat before fires and pentagrams, and they speak in dead dialects. They struggle with complex intonations of the Kabbalah. The journey is arduous.

A few have bathed in blood, and the ghosts of their victims prance inside the shadows of the empty wards. Lucretia Murteen has become a nun—a bride of the Flying Walendas—and she can see the needy apparitions from her empty socket. Sister Lucretia says she hears babies crying in the nursery.

I am technically a monk, by proxy. My name is still on the building and Abbott Earl feels that I am a benefactor, at least, if not a true believer.

I attend the occasional meal with them, and observe their rules while I'm among the order. I wear a cowl and robes with thistles and barbs woven into them. I chant. I only speak between sixth and seventh hour. I remain chaste. I do not take the holy name of Walenda in vain.

Anything is possible here, as it is on the wire in the savage wind.

JONAH recites the names of symphonies, poems and sit-coms, from the core of his third of that brain. It's almost all he can do on his own, but that doesn't matter. His words are passionate and true. The execution, the intent, the subtleties of tone and finesse of his tongue add new depths of expression. For Sarah, who sleeps with Fred down the hall. *"The Lovesong of J. Alfred Prufrock, The Odd Couple, please, Barney Miller,*

In a Disguised Graveyard, Toccata, Mandoline Concerto...Because I could not stop for Death, please oh please, Three's Company, I Love Lucy, Waltz of the Flowers, Liebestraum, Gilligan's Island, Will and Grace, Do Not Go Gentle into that Good Night...McHale's Navy, Burns and Allen, The Moon and the Yew Tree, Seinfeld, Adagio, Arrival of the Queen of Sheba, please come to me, I await you, I am always waiting, you see..."

He is sobbing madly, the tears corrupting his throat, while Sebastian cackles in whispers and Cole remains oddly silent.

A WIDE but dull moon doesn't have what it takes to illuminate the inside of my truck. Whoever she is, she's doing all right in my lap without me. She smells of death, but that doesn't matter a hell of a lot at the moment. Her hair is a fiery red that might only be orange in the daylight, but for now it is a mass of bobbing flame that spills across my belly to my knees.

She's producing noises that could be ecstasy, or perhaps this is only an agonizing murder. It's hard to tell. There weren't any women in the bar tonight, so how did she find me? The woods. I think she moved on me from the woods. She drags her nails down my legs and back up again, making other little motions as if she's scratching sparse but powerful sentences into my skin. I try to make them out. It's a cursive script with well-defined curves, crossed t's and dotted i's and hanging g's. Lots of passive verbs. There are a meager number of semi-colons but a fair amount of emphasis is drawn to certain words via italics.

Each new section, with chapter heading, begins with capitalization done in an ostentatious biblical-style calligraphy. There are extensive footnotes designating sets and subsets for further referencing.

As my orgasm draws closer she begins writing much faster, and we're in the middle of a significant race that carries great consequence. Suddenly I'm filled with a sense of despondency. I know I need to beat her to the finish before she can complete her incantations and invoke some other form of dread.

I buck wildly into her mouth—what might be her mouth—but she's no longer using her tongue for my purpose. Only her own. She's talking to me or somebody else, *something* else drawing closer through the vast dark woods surrounding the parking lot. She repeats key phrases—names, clauses, entreaties, demands, and she keeps making more and more promises.

The statements in my flesh have ignited, and the truck grows brighter. Her face remains wreathed in shadow, hidden in a blackness that will always have sharp teeth. Trees bend in the wind, leaves writhing and whirling on burning fetid breath.

I pull her face closer to me, grinding my hips forward and hoping to make a mess of her penmanship, but she's studied and trained too long for my ploy to work. She's got great discipline for this.

That's fine as I grunt and hold tightly to her cold, stiff hair. My cum streams down her throat, if she has a throat, if the mouth and hands are connected to anything at all. Claws tighten on my hips—it was a close race but I've won, and managed to escape another trap.

A heavy presence recedes into the brush. She continues sucking until my sweat has dried, my skin cooled, and my cock is hard again.

We proceed once more, perhaps to a different aftermath.

CHAPTER THREE

DRABS has his clothes on and we're in his kitchen drinking coffee. He's all right for the time being, a man of the earth and not of air, with only one tongue. He's set aside God for the moment, or maybe it's God who's tossed him aside. Perhaps Christ has finally taken some pity on him. Drabs is on a sugar high, pouring heaping spoonfuls into the slightly tart, boiling coffee.

The morning sunlight gushes over his shoulder, making his beaded black skin shine with a certain purity. He wants to talk about Maggie and yet he doesn't want to speak of her—we've been torn like this since we were nine years old. While I've grown accustomed to it, even comfortable in a way, he hasn't and never will. Small talk is out of the question, and there are too many devastating and exhausting troubles for us to find any easy topic.

I know if I ask about the geek I'll bring the wrath of the Lord down upon one of us. I make an opening but he's got something else he wants to bring out.

"They found a child today, down in the bottoms."

My heart is suddenly snarled in my rib cage. My

chest throbs painfully. "How long has he been there?"

"I didn't say it was a 'he.' Just so happens it was a girl. Maybe six years old or so. Seven, eight."

"Did you see her?"

"No, I heard."

"Who found her?"

"Dodi's mother, that Velma Coots. Imagine it if you can—" I can and let him go on. His grin is harsh and humorless. "—here the conjure woman comes, crawling over creeks and down through the ditches, hunting for her roots and berries and insects for purposes untold. Covered in muck up to her thighs and holding a handful of swamp moss and snake skin, and she finds a child laid out on the flat rock."

My heart his hitting bone now and I can feel the vibrations in my back teeth. "They were at the flat rock?"

"Just as I said."

Designs and forces are drawing closer together. I feel as if I should understand it by now, but I still can't make anything out clearly.

Drabs and I had found the flat rock just like almost every kid did, although not all of us talked about it or ever went back again. It was a slab, perhaps a shrine or a sacrificial stone, built centuries ago, with channels running down its length to siphon off the purifying oils and blood. Some of the townsfolk thought it should be destroyed, broken into bits and the dust mixed with salt and scattered across the bottoms. Others, like my father, believed it should be moved yet preserved, studied at the university and considered as an archeological discovery worth some note.

Still others decided it should be used.

And it *had* been used over the years, usually by

granny witches who consecrated scarecrows and goats there, hoping to appease an elemental force that lived on in our faiths and practices, down in the mists of antiquity.

Bodies are sometimes found there as well—elderly who die of natural causes, kids who go to bed at night in their beds and wake up laid out on the flat rock with no idea how they got there. On occasion just a bone or two. Usually they belong to an animal, but not always. The stone remains in the deep woods of Potts County, not too far from the river, and no matter the argument, it will always be there.

"What happened?" I ask.

I wait because when Drabs is like this, in his right mind and exceptionally focused, full of intent, he makes you wait. We have another cup of coffee, letting the day rise around us. Noon approaches. Shadows loom as we face each other. Someone walking in might think we are relaxed.

Soon, though, his knees start to jump, fingers tapping as he unravels strand by strand. The nervous tics appear in his face one after the other as the surging sugar works through him.

"So," he says. "Where was I?"

"Dodi's mother, hands full of swamp grass, snake skin, berries and so forth, at the flat rock and finding the six, seven or possibly eight-year-old girl."

"Yes."

I watch him going farther away from me, inch by inch, button by button, as he undoes his shirt. I haven't brought the Holy Spirit down on him this time. It's the beauty of the morning, the taste of too much sweetness.

I need to hear the rest. I stand and yank the table

aside, toppling it, and then grab Drabs by his shirt front. I hold it shut with my left hand. I clamp my right on his forehead as if trying to keep his thoughts inside his steaming brain. "You can roll around naked in the ravine all you want to later, Drabs."

"No, no, I—"

"Now, tell me about the girl. This could be important."

"Why so?"

"Come on," I urge.

Even with the sugar and caffeine rush in effect, as the tongues are coming for him, his eyes center on me and I feel him coiling back into himself a little. He's safe for a few seconds more while I keep his clothes on. He blinks as if seeing me for the first time. He says, "Velma Coots goes to inspect the body, unsure if it's actually a child."

"Unsure?"

"Possibly a well-made scarecrow, you know how they get. But this one here, it's got a large lollipop, one of those all-day suckers."

"I've got it."

"A rainbow, it's a rainbow of concentric colors, twirling in the light, spinning, spinning..."

"Stay with me."

"...with that Velma Coots dropping her mystical wares, berries and critters and so forth, as she rushes forward, yelling."

"Because it's not a goddamn scarecrow."

"Of course not, it's a child. A girl, as I said. And this girl, roused by the screams, rises from the flat rock—"

"She's alive?"

"—and holds her all-day sucker before her in a gesture of defense, like that, like that, with two days of grime on her, no food at all except this lollipop. Unable to recall her name, or maybe simply incapable of speaking it."

"But she's all right?"

He nods once, searching my eyes as I look into his. The hand I have on his forehead is beginning to heat up as if I've got it on a stove. "Yes," Drabs says, "she's fine, and staying in town with Lily while the sheriff tries to find out who the child is and where she belongs."

I release his shirt and stand close by as the tongues come at him from everywhere. He spins and jerks away as if someone is flicking matches at him. The tongues lick out his identity until he's nothing more than a vessel shrieking in the non-language of martyrs. The Holy Spirit clambers inside him as he squirms on the kitchen floor. There are too many sharp corners in here so I open the back door and let him wriggle out into the yard, terrifying a hawk in flight above us. He spasms beneath sweet gum and mimosa, scaring cormorants standing in the brush.

I start back towards my truck. Before I leave he says one more thing that I can understand.

I stop and turn. His voice is clear and serene even while he thrashes. "The carnival is coming."

ONCE every week or so I spend a day at the mill.

You can feel the vehemence the workers have for the place, and you can understand how the mill itself feeds on that malice to keep going on, year after year.

Sometimes there is no place to put your anger and frustration, and sometimes, luckily, there is.

Paul, the foreman, knows exactly how to handle me. He says good morning and then stays the hell away. My office—which had been my father's and grandfather's and great-grandfather's before me, bears no sign of any of us. The walls are not scarred or blemished, the century-old desk appears new and perfect. There is nothing to be seen of ownership or tradition. The dust in here is the same dust from the last eighty years, and I breathe it in as they breathed it in, and then breathe it out again.

This office is actually one of the few places where I feel content. I stand at the window overlooking the factory floor and watch the rows of employees using their hands the way my family taught them. The patterns are complex but repetitive, the thrum of machinery deadening but also soothing.

My great-grandfather instituted a no-talking policy on the floor that lasted for seventy-five years until I changed it. I had to fill out thirty-seven insurance forms in order to do so. It wasn't that he believed production would suffer if the workers talked to one another, but he knew that the number of injuries would increase if they didn't fully concentrate on their tasks. That machinery could tear a man's arm off in three seconds. And great-granddad was right. Reports of injuries have gone up—fingers lost in gears, punctures and lacerated tendons and shattered knuckles. There was even a death here eighteen months ago, the first since the mill began operating.

Still, my forefathers never sat at those benches, performing the same murderously menial and tedious job every day, and I have. I spent all four of my high school years there among the men and women, learning and operating each machine in turn, without talking. With absolutely nothing but the staccato pounding and beating metal and fluorescent lighting to keep me from plunging into the endless depths of my own thoughts and insane boredom.

They hold me in esteem, or at least they pretend to. They wave and I wave back. There are twelve hundred of them down there and only me up above them. They grow self-conscious beneath my gaze: not just as laborers but as my neighbors. I make them blush.

The mill pays out a high insurance premium but now there are voices to be heard again above the clanking cogs. Chatter rises to the distant rafters. Chuckles and gossip and the retelling of bad jokes, an expression of human need and primordial instinct. It's only humane.

Giggles and flirting, discussions of hair care products and wrinkle cream. They grunt about fishing and hunting, that terrible football game last night, the nonfat potato chip, the scraping of gums, bad milk, infantile paralysis—and more, always more—Sears & Roebuck, political platforms, that bizarre lesion on your back shaped like the governor's profile, frying of catfish, the praising of Jesus, the praising of Walenda—and still more, because there must be more, and of course you can't turn away—at the opening of old heartaches, and Gloria took the kids and is living with that car mechanic on the other side of town, wha's his name, Verbal Raynes, that's the one yeah the lousy prick—and he is, you know he is, and it's killing her husband Harry—but you can't be calling him the prick, Harry, ain't his fault Gloria left you, it's been six weeks already—that ain't the fucking point—and it's not the fucking point.

There are screams, it's true.

They've come to be expected and, at least on some level, even hoped for as diversion. We wish for them.

MY mother had many dreams that are now mine.

In a recurring one, I am walking through a field carrying an infant, side by side with Maggie. She wears a sun dress and bonnet. We are standing in wheat. There's no wheat for three states in any direction, but that's what my mother dreams about. The baby gives a toothless smile and holds out his chubby hands as if the whole world is a rare and precious thing for him to hold. My wife glances at me, radiant with the autumn sun, her hair curling out from beneath the bonnet and struck by the sunlight in such a way that her features are suddenly blazing, as natural and perfect as the season itself.

Sometimes I wake up crying, with my brothers leaning over my bed, staring and weeping with me.

LILY the repressed schoolteacher has real initiative, and she finds me at the mill. No one has ever found me here, or needed to find me here, so I'm a little shocked to see her coming up the stairs with the girl in tow.

"Thomas, we need your help," Lily says, sitting in the chair at the front of my desk. It may be the very first time anybody has ever sat there.

We are in the convergence corridor now. I can feel it quite strongly, this gathering of energy. The girl from the flat rock, the warnings from Drabs, the talk of Gloria leaving Harry for Verbal, my mother's unfolding dreams, the ghost of my father, and the coming of the carnival.

Whoever said the kid was seven years old saw her at a distance. She's at least thirteen or fourteen and looks rather ridiculous holding an all-day sucker. I can see how the mistake has been made though. She's wearing a younger girl's school outfit: bobby socks, tiny plastic black shoes that belong on a doll, and her hair is in pig-tails for Christ's sake. She's confused and wide-eyed, gawking all around the room and down below at the rest of the mill. When her gaze settles on me it's like she's stabbing me in the belly. Sometimes you know when someone wants something from you. I'm waiting for her to lick the lollipop but she doesn't. Her knuckles are white around the stick as she angles the sucker like a sword. She cocks her head cutely and I wonder what the hell is going on.

"What can I do?" I ask.

Lily has decided to live the stereotype. She wears glasses with thick black frames, her hair always kept up in a tightly knotted bun. She has a penchant for oversized clothing, large blouses and sweaters, lengthy skirts, a lack of form. She does this to hide the true nature of her beautiful body from herself and from the licentious men of Kingdom Come.

Lily used to fuck me down into the floorboards beneath the bed with her massive tits mashed into my mouth until I turned a light shade of blue, her cunt alive and starving. She is dichotomy itself, and neither role is any more or less real, although I definitely like the one who fucks a lot better.

Her staunch persona is in effect. One of Lily's hands flutters about as if she were brandishing a ruler or a piece of chalk at a map, pointing out the Gobi Desert, the Pyramid of Cheops, the corner where the woman in the red dress led Dillinger to his death.

She says, "Do you know of our situation here?"

"Not really," I tell her.

"The circumstances surrounding this little girl. I call her Eve simply because we must call her something."

"Yes."

"Well, Sheriff Burke hasn't been able to find her parents yet or where she comes from or how it is she's gotten here. If she's been kidnapped and brought across state lines this could be the responsibility of the F.B.I., but we really don't know where to turn in order to help Eve."

I look at the girl and she appears completely oblivious to us now. "Has she spoken at all?"

"No, not a word."

"Is it something physical or has she been traumatized?"

"Doctor Jenkins isn't sure. There's no immediate signs of abuse. She appears perfectly healthy in every other regard. There's always a chance she'll snap out of it, whatever 'it' might actually be. I'm horrified to think what that poor girl might have been through."

It makes me uncomfortable talking about the girl as if she wasn't there, as she glances at me. Everything about her makes me uneasy—those clothes, the swell of her pubescent breast, that damn all-day sucker with its concentric colors winding me into its syrupy abyss. Eve wanders onto the platform outside the door and waves down at the workers the way I do, and they wave back.

Lily's stern manner is beginning to turn me on the way it used to. "What can I do?"

"I'd like to hire a private investigator."

"All right."

"It might prove costly. A P.I. could be on this case for weeks or even months, and wind up with little or nothing to show for his efforts."

"That's fine. Is she staying with you?"

"Yes, there's enough room in my house and truthfully, I enjoy the company. We're making do, and she seems to have already grown quite at ease." Her gaze is downcast, with a nice flush already creeping up her neck. I imagine those big red knockers bobbing all around while I take her from behind. She knows what I'm thinking and her hands flit to her glasses, to keep them on, to yank them off. She says, "Do you want to make the arrangements or shall I?"

"I will. I'll get an agency to start working on this immediately."

"Thank you, Thomas."

"Of course, Lily."

I call Paul the foreman up to the office and tell him that perhaps Eve would like a tour of the mill. He knows better than to frown. He takes Eve by the hand, quickly becoming entranced by the circling colors of that all-day sucker. Paul gets a bit woozy and I have to grip his shoulder to snap him out of it. He leads her downstairs among the awful machinery and curious people who call her the flat rock girl in whispers.

We defeat the dead air of ages as Lily and I move, in spasms, up onto the desk naked and glistening. We tear gouts from the wooden floor and walls, with nails and teeth, leaving marks for the rest of history to see.

SARAH is not accustomed to being wooed and she

likes the attention. In the deep night, when Fred has finally fallen into his fitful sleep and cocaine night-mares, she comes to our bedroom. She is apprehensive, which only makes sense. Jonah is charming in his own way, and the timbre of his voice coming from all three throats of my brothers is enthralling. She enjoys his poetry and selfless attentions, even if she doesn't know which body is actually his.

"And in the aggression of our loss we find, another draped flattery at your feet, as roses and accolades and murmurs all day are cast once again, into the saltless seas of our impertinent memories."

Sarah does not join them in bed. There's room for her now that Dodi has taken to sleeping with me or alone in one of the empty bedrooms on the third floor. Sarah sits on the floor, her head eased back against the edge of the mattress, sighing after each of Jonah's stanzas. Despite their physical disfigurement, the voice from those three throats is quite splendid.

I usually enjoy listening, but tonight I'm not in the mood.

I wander the house, feeling the breeze as I step across each open window in every hall. Downstairs the mantel appears strange, and it takes me a moment to realize that the framed photo of my parents is missing.

There's a noise at the end of the corridor. I follow the sound. To my surprise, I see that Fred is lying awake. Usually he stays up for three paranoia-wracked days in a row and then crashes hard, but he must be snorting so much now that it's bounced him back to life. I'm shirtless and he stares at what might be my sister in my side. The feminine features at my ribs having shifted slightly into a grimace.

He talks to the face. "She's leaving me."

"Yes, I think so," I tell him.

"We've been together for almost two years, and now she's dropping me, like that, all the way out here in the fucking boonies."

"Maybe it's best this way."

"Fuck no it's not best like this! How can you even say that? Listen, we had plans, we were going places. She was going to write screenplays and I'd get the financing and produce and direct them. That's the way it was. But this?...the hell is this? She's cutting loose and leaving me for that goddamn obscene creature!"

"Only one third of it. My brother Jonah."

"I don't care what you call it! Haven't you seen the way it moves and what it does? Jesus, it isn't human!"

He hops up out of bed, nothing but tendon, muscle, bone and a few dug-in ticks because he's always too high to burn them off. No fat, no extra pieces or persons. He's bursting with a manic tension, each vein raised. He rushes to the bureau and begins ferreting about, tossing aside clothes and empty vials, sections of scripts. He spills talcum powder and baby laxative, and a white mushroom cloud explodes into the air, leaving traces on the ceiling.

Fred is shaking his head like a swimmer with water in his ear, but he can't get out the sound, the infection. I feel a great pity for him even though he's such an asshole. He scowls at my ribs. "You think I'm not man enough to keep my woman? You think I won't fight for her?"

"There's no need to. You've got to accept the fact that she's leaving you. The war is over. You've lost."

"Like hell I have."

Like hell, he has. Fred has now become expendable. He has no reason or purpose to remain with us and probably never really did. Stepping foot in this house was like getting caught in quicksand, and the more he struggled the deeper set he got until he couldn't get away again. Sarah, though, will stay behind. To what end, I don't know, but that's for her to decide.

Fred sold off most of his belongings days ago for more drugs. The video camera and the DAT recorder are long gone, and so are all of the worthwhile effects from the house—the television, stereo, all the petty cash, my watch and other jewelry. None of it is important to me except the framed photo of my parents that he lifted tonight.

I search the room while he continues to strew items everywhere. We're both digging and rutting around. He looks over and says, "What are you doing? Hey you, what's your name again? Listen, that's mine! Take your hands off that. That's mine. Hey—"

The photo is halfway free of the frame and the glass is cracked. I turn to go and Fred pulls out one of our kitchen knives from under the mattress. He's even more disconnected than I thought. He looks down at the face and asks, "What was that? What'd you say to me, you bitch?"

I try to listen, but there's nothing.

He's fast but awkward. The knife slashes down but he misses me by six inches. I don't even need to step aside. He tries again, stabbing for my ribs, for my sister's pouting face, and I jerk left, catching his wrist and bending it backwards, further and further until he drops the blade. I keep going until the popping and cracking of small bones grows loud enough to drown out Jonah's recital.

I slap a hand over his mouth. Fred is screeching beneath the palm I use to cover his slippery lips. I keep the pressure up, twisting, feeling the hairline fracture working up his ulna inch by inch.

His agonized, horrified eyes keep gazing towards the face as I hiss into his ear, "Listen, I've been recutting your coke with an even better crystal than you're used to. You were stepping on yours too much. If you're going to do something then do it right. You're leaving tonight, Fred, and you're going without Sarah."

He bucks like a dying fish and I slip my hand aside so I can hear him. "No! My arm! Hey, no, you—"

"My brother loves her and she's starting to fall for him, I think. Get over the fact that it's a little weird."

"A little! Ow! Oh God...help, listen...."

It will finish badly when she dries out, I suppose, and probably end with madness, but almost everything does. I tell him, "Be pleased. It provides reassurance, a new hope for all. Take heart in that."

I let go of him. Even though his arm is broken, the relief of my turning him loose overwhelms him and Fred groans and pants on his knees. I stuff a thousand bucks in his pocket, drag him down the hall, and shove him through the front door out across the porch. He bounces down the steps onto the lawn, moaning in tune with the cadence of Jonah's poetry and all the loons and katydids.

Maggie, huddled in the willows, maintains her vigil.

THUNDER hangs heavily in the furious clouds to the east as the storm approaches. The river is already in a frenzy, half a foot higher than normal. The jut of cruel chins is outlined by lightning, and the sky is the color of a three day old bruise. Electrical surges burn out and explode bulbs all over the house, sending shards of glass soaring. Even the dog kicker must be staying in. No size twelve tracks are found in the mud, no dirty prints have been left on fur. Dogs are accepting treats from their owners again, showing a little tail-wagging. But they continue to howl, and you know there's a reason.

When the rains finally come, the world is given a new perspective. Not whitewashed or cleansed, but slickly covered over and gleaming. Water pulses beneath windowpanes. It crawls across trees and houses, swallowing and drinking us in. You watch it arching over steeples and cliffs and the cabbage palms, buffeting, constantly beating and vying for your attention.

Trucks going by tear up the brutal din with separate gentler sounds: splashes, splurges, crunches and whines. Anything is better than the pitter-patter and constant thrum of wind coming for you. Broadhead skinks skitter down walls, leaping into the water. The lightning is frantic and raging, that sudden charge making your hair bristle and skin tighten. Your ears pop. Fires erupt in the woods but the downpour immediately snuffs them out. You almost want to see the wild burning because it's something that can exist, momentarily, in conflict with the storm.

The parking lot of Leadbetter's is abruptly littered with corpses. Three drunks in two nights are found drowned in sixteen inch puddles to one side of the curb where the grade dips. Two-hundred-and-thirty pound men with forty-inch beer guts are discovered drifting with their key chains in hand, slowly circling a stopped drain. You pass out during a storm like this and you're dead.

Shanty houses in the bog town are consumed in avalanches of mud and slide into the swamp. Ramshackle hovels at the edge of Potts County simply fall to pieces and families are forced to move into their trucks and chicken coops.

Dodi, who used to enjoy dancing in the rain, running around the yard and begging me to join her on the swing, comes to loathe the gurgling, sluicing water thudding at the roof. She can't sleep and lies awake crimped at the foot of the bed. She wants company and I move with her into a different room, watching her nervously curl and uncurl.

She doesn't often seem to mind being traded away by her mother, but tonight seems to be an exception. Dodi scowls at the ceiling. Velma Coots knows spells to keep a tempest like this at bay, potions intended to hold the hidden evils back. The thumping and tapping at the walls is like the hammering of the damned waiting to get inside. Why they'd want to, I don't know.

She covers her ears and lets out a muffled cry, the sheets twisting tightly around her lithe body, each flawless curve shown off. "I can't stand much more of this, Thomas. I can feel the demons out there, roving about."

"It'll pass in another day or two."

"Storms like this one don't just leave on their own, you've got to do something to run it off. It's a storm of souls, the granny ladies say. The dead want back in and they've brought all the sins of the people along with them. Mama would know what to do."

"Do you want to visit her? I'll take you in the morning."

"I ain't going out there." She speaks in a way that makes it sound like the rains, and what's in them, have come specifically for her or for me. "Can't you feel how badly it wants us?"

"Us?

"All of us."

We can't call her mother because Velma Coots doesn't have a phone. That's uncommon even in Potts County, but not unheard of. "It's late, Dodi, try to sleep. Maybe by morning this will have blown over."

"You have to go, Thomas."

"What?"

"You gotta go."

"Where?"

"To see Mama and find out what to do."

I pull the blankets around us. "If there's really something that could be done, wouldn't she be doing it already?"

"She might need some help. Mama's strong in her ways but she can't protect all of Kingdom Come by her lonesome. It's been a labor for her so far, and it's getting worse."

I don't sneer and I don't question. If I chose to scoff and dispute what goes on in Potts County I'd never stop, and I'd wind up like my father. "The other conjure women can join her."

Branches scratch at the shingles, wood clapping on wood. It's a familiar sound, and one I like, but Dodi snaps up as if a child killer is just outside. Sweat courses down her neck, dappling my legs. Her fear is intoxicating and erotic but also sobering. I want to take her roughly but a detached terror is filling the room. I wonder what's going on between Sarah and my brothers, and if they can feel this too. Or whether they all sleep blithely and dream of each other. I think I hear talking.

Dodi moves forward across my chest, the wet sheet drawing unpleasantly over us now. Beads of sweat hang off her nipples. I want her desperately, and I don't want her at all.

"Maybe it's got to do with that little gal from the flat rock, and what happened there," she says. "Or what hasn't happened yet and still needs to be done."

"What do you mean?"

I've always known that Velma Coots didn't give Dodi to me in payment for fixing a goddamn roof and digging screw worms out of a couple of sick cows. There was another agenda to the transaction. There usually is. When Dodi looks at me in this fashion, I remember once more it's true, and I realize she's actually here to spy on me for some reason. There's genuine panic in her flitting eyes, and the last piece of the masquerade slips from her as she trembles in my arms. I can see the purpose, but not the objective.

"What's your mother want from me?" I ask.

"You got power, Thomas, more than any of the granny witches. More than all of them. There's power in names and it was your family that named this town. In one way, you *are* the town, and we're you."

"Dodi, I think you're getting a little carried away here—"

But she isn't. I hold her on the bed for a long while until her head droops and her breathing eases. Her skin dries with strange outlines of salt streaks. She falls asleep to the muted whispers of Sarah and Jonah down the hall. I let her slide from me and cover her with a blanket.

I take the truck into town, driving carefully along

the flooded roads. I've got to stop several times in order to shift debris so I can ride by. When I get to Velma Coots' shack she's standing in her doorway, glowering at the folds of swarming rain, waiting for me.

"'Bout time you got here," she says. "Was starting to think you weren't gonna show."

I step inside and I'm somewhat gratified to see that even in this torrential downpour and heavy wind, the roof job I did is holding up. A brass cauldron in the fireplace spews noxious fumes and sloshing black liquid. A short curved blade lies on a table nearby.

"What the hell do you want from me?" I ask.

"Jest a little blood and vinegar, there, in the pot."

"Vinegar?"

"Some of yer seed."

"My seed?"

"Sperm."

"You've got to be shittin' me."

She isn't, and her expression is so contorted that the hinges of her jaw look like they're in the wrong places. "Evil's come looking for us. It's here to stay one way or another. The bad is just gonna get worse. The demons and the spirits, they up in arms and on the loose. You know that, and you believe it, otherwise you wouldn't be here." She purses her lips and gives me a slow once over, as if this will be the last time she ever sees me. "'Sides, the carnival will be coming through soon. We ain't got much time at all."

"What's that got to do with anything?"

"Everybody's got sacrifices to make," she says. "Or don't you know that already?"

I shake my head but it's all right. I take up the blade and cut my hand open over the boiling brew.

Where my blood strikes the liquid it hisses and spits. The flames bend and sputter as if drinking. I remember my father's failures to change these ancient ways, and how his defeats and near-sightedness eventually drove him into the one hope of Kingdom Come, his own miserable mill.

Velma Coots gives me a scarf and I bind my wound.

"Now, your seed."

"No."

"I need it!"

"Sorry, I have more use for my vinegar than you do."

She starts hopping in place. "You got to. The magic won't work proper without it!"

"Do your best."

She takes the blade and holds it out towards my belly as if she plans to use it on me. The fire reflects in the sheen of my blood coating the knife. I glare at her, waiting to see if she's really going to make this kind of move. She's castrated a thousand pigs in her life. Rain crashes harder and still the roof holds against it. I can take pride in that, if nothing else, why the hell not.

She lets loose a snarl and stabs the knife into a wooden table. "Then whatever happens from here on out is on your conscience, Thomas, you hear that? It's on your head."

"Of course it is," I say. "So what else is new?"

Chapter Four

SOMEONE is calling my name.

She needs help and is begging adorably, the way we all like.

In the night I awaken to find my brothers talking to the face. They sway in the darkness, a shambling mass of bodies—of body. Sebastian is delirious with fury, his complaints coming from three throats, hitting three different notes, harmonizing well with a little doo-wop shuffle going on. They glare at each other, stuffed with devotion and anger and regret, each third of that brain filled with memories and needs.

Sarah isn't here and neither is Dodi, but I feel a female nearby, one that makes me possessive. They want her, and they'll go through me to get her. I listen, hoping to hear her voice, but there's nothing now but the cruel whispers of my brothers, the feel of lips playing against my side. It's too dark to know which of them is kissing her. Perhaps they're taking turns, each attending the face in his own manner.

I try to enter myself, aware of every breath, the singular beating of my sole heart. The chill of my belly, and the cold pressure of their mouths. I go further inside, hoping to discover muscles that might be making her eyes blink, small indented nostrils breathing deeply, misplaced cheekbones, lovely earlobes.

There isn't anybody. It's a bruise or a scar. Cole is weeping and Sebastian, in his hate, bites into my side. The storm is no match for his own fever. Pain erupts, but I'm not certain it's mine. Blood runs thickly down to the mattress. They scurry away, one of them laughing as they move, in spasms, with a whirl of limbs and clashing purpose.

I get up and turn on the light. Rain thumps and the house creaks and settles. My brothers are under a sheet, flinching, pretending to sleep, baiting me. It gets like this sometimes.

The vast and overpowering noise of a massive tree toppling fills the room. It sounds as if the whole house is about to be crushed beneath a hundred tons of history. The rafters rock and the pounding rain withdraws into vacuum, the sudden displacement bringing us to total silence for an instant before the thunderous blast.

The oak falls directly past the window. A million branches undulate like snakes crawling by, striking the ground in an earsplitting explosion of mud and splintered timber.

I tear the sheet aside and grab hold of Sebastian, lifting his stunted frame and taking the others along too. The mouths are going at once, all of them talking at the same time with a dissonance of words, the tributary voice, the sub-text and cacophony of tone and meaning.

They make no sense and neither do I. I'm yelling, but I'm not sure what about. I'm leaking all over, and I've got my own rage. This is when it's good, when everyone is at his best. I try to look my brother in the eye but I can't, he's forever turned inwards facing the others, glowering at Cole who continues to sob.

"Why did you bite me?"

"I didn't," Sebastian says from their throats.

"I'm bleeding."

"No, you're not."

The blood drips and patters on the floor, loud in the room even with the wind bashing at the house. Is he being purposefully dense or is he playing word games?...telling me that another—the face that may be my sister—is the one who is bitten and bleeding? Is he trying to wrangle me into an admission? In that forebrain anything is possible.

"It hurt."

"Not you it didn't."

I want to hit him but I'd break my hand on that three-fold skull. I go to the bathroom to clean myself up, searching each shade and line of my side. I'm looking for the familiar face but see only Sebastian's teeth marks.

Perhaps she's with them now—adhered on a chest, growing in an arm pit, or dangling off a kneecap—beloved and finally wanted, and so much the luckier for it.

DRAGGING his past behind him like a mill-stone, the private eye meets me in my office.

His name is Nick Stiel and two months ago his wife of eight years died of leukemia. He says it flatly without any emotion. His eyes are half-lidded as if it's an ordeal for him to open them all the way. His hands are slender but his wrists are surprisingly thick. The watchband is too tight, and course black hair sprouts from around it. His palms are callused, the first two knuckles scarred and distended. He's studied martial arts for years. One of the Japanese disciplines, I'd guess. None of the spiritual doctrine has helped him to get over her loss.

I've given him one file containing a full report on the situation concerning Eve and another on the dog kicker. There's also a map of the county, names and home addresses of everybody currently involved, photos of Eve, keys to a 4x4 wagon I rented for him, and a three thousand dollar retainer.

"Why me?" he asks.

"You concentrate on lost child cases and you've got a high rate of success."

"In Los Angeles. This is whole different world."

"You ain't kidding."

He blinks, attempting to think it through. He knows it doesn't feel right but he's too distracted by his wife's death to get past the fog. His heartbreak is so apparent I can tell he'll get along well in Kingdom Come. If he tried to beguile the people of Potts County, or lie to them or provoke or bully or trade witty banter, he wouldn't get so much as a shrug from any of them.

"You don't have a lost child here," he says. "You've got a found one."

"A considerably harder job for you, I'd guess."

"It is," he confesses. "Missing children cases almost always involve a parent, family member, neighbor, or pedophile with a prison record. It's a matter of investigating the home situation and canvassing the neighborhood for suspects."

"The same might hold true here."

"It might," Stiel says. "If she was brought here for a reason."

"It's a working theory."

Thunder performs a contrapuntal to our voices, booming during pauses, in a slow but rhythmic collision like waves striking the shore. He's unnerved by the noise, and after three days of it, so am I. He's so emotionally battered that he'll be able to deal with the townsfolk's customs and the bad attitude of the granny witches. There's distrust among their kind, but anyone with eyes like his has a better chance of being welcomed.

"She still doesn't remember anything?" he asks.

"That's what she says."

He nods. "You sound as if you don't believe her."

"I suppose it's possible."

"But unlikely."

"Yes."

Nick Stiel moves slowly, shifting in his seat, facing the window as rivulets of intense rain streak sideways across the glass. "You know these people. Are there any suspects?"

"I'm not even sure a crime's been committed."

He looks at the list of names. "What the hell is the Holy Order of Flying Waldendas?"

"A monastery nearby."

"Sounds more like a cult."

"I suppose it is."

"How might they be involved?"

"Seekers are drawn to the abbey."

"Seekers?"

"As I said. People looking for something in their lives. God, faith, a retreat from the cities maybe. Some stay on but most don't. This girl was found out at a place we call the flat rock. It's an ancient slab and might have some pagan or pseudo-religious significance."

Something very much like a smile nearly lifts the edges of his lips. "You really believe that?"

"My father did."

Despite his current mental state, he's subtle, superior, and already on the case. Stiel still has his instincts. He can ask me anything but knows that I might be the culprit myself, playing games with lives, looking to be captured. He's judging reactions and trying hard to get a bead on me.

"What do you think happened?" he asks.

I could tell him that the girl was brought out to the flat rock in order to be sacrificed to an old god or a quite possibly a new one. Or that she's a demon in disguise. Or a nymphet who's left a trail of smashed middle-aged men exactly like him in her wake. She's only playing eight. Eve could be thirteen or eighteen or eternal.

"That's what I'm paying you to find out, Stiel."

I can see him sticking around in Kingdom Come whether he solves this matter or not. He'll have to spend a lot of time interviewing the girl and talking with Lily, his misery alive within him but his lust making itself known. Each day in Lily's small empty house, sitting in front of her bare walls and facing that stern glance, watching the vague proportions of her body. Always seeing more of her, the many sides of Lily, that slope of her big tits, the turn of her ankle, the way she snatches her glasses off her face and grips the plastic arm between her teeth, tongue darting.

In six weeks they'll probably be married or dead, and if Eve's true nature is not discovered, he might find himself becoming her father.

HUDDLING in the dim recesses of Leadbetter's, not caring about the lightning strikes in the hills or the fact that the floods are now high enough to cover their license plates, they continue to meet and share pain. This is custom. This is ritual.

Verbal Raynes, having his third pitcher of beer, throws his mug against the wall with the wild boar's head on it and shouts, "God damn it, I wish Gloria would go back to her husband!"

The others respond with deep sympathy and soothing, comforting words. "Fuck that bitch!"

Verbal scratches at his three-day beard and considers. His contemplation takes him farther inside the almost empty pitcher of beer, and the bartender gives him a new mug and charges him for the busted one. The boys attend.

"She say she miss Harry?"

"No, keeps telling me she don't ever want to see him again."

"Well, now, that ain't a good sign, I'm thinking."

"Not what I was hoping for, truth be known," Verbal says.

"Yup."

They, like most men, are men of myth and mediocrity. They carry with them the fables of their commonplace grandfathers and the blood of warriors and drunks. Over the years, they've had to scrape their broken fathers off the back porch and put cold compresses on their mothers' busted noses. They've awoken in un-mopped kitchen corners beneath the scowls of wives who've been failed early by life. This is their heritage and legacy.

"Her kids move in with you too?"

"All three of them."

"Three! Goddamn!"

"Jesus, take me now, Lord."

"Verbal, you is a doomed man. No wonder that Harry ain't looking so glum anymore these days."

"The lucky bastard."

"She at least still good in bed?"

"No more," Verbal tells them. "Like lying a'top a fresh caught bass."

"Deeder done that once. On accident, a'course. Don't look at me like that. Me and him, we was—"

"It's only been three weeks, you'd think she coulda kept warm a little longer than that!"

"It's a sad affair, I'd say."

"The hell was you and Deeder doing with them poor bass again?"

"I done told you it was an accident."

"But the game warden said—"

"Who's word you gonna take? His or mine? Wasn't rightly doing nothing to them, mind you, it's jest that when Deeder—"

"Let's have another drink."

"And fill 'em to the top this time."

Mugs high, the dim light catching in the speckled foam. "To Deeder and his Large Mouth Bass, may God forgive his profane soul."

The women circle and dance alone or in pairs to the lonely strains of guitars and banjos on the juke box. Even if they listen to the men, which they never do, they wouldn't hear them. A man's dread is not their dread. There are dilemmas that cannot be equated or solved. His pitiful cares and frets have no real standing in comparison, they think. Look at the stretch marks and wrinkling upper lip and loosening chin, the ass that hasn't quite dropped.

Smoke is so heavy in the room that you could get stuck in it like barbed-wire.

Women coil in close, being eyed, laughing too loudly but without any humor, attracting the wrong kind of attention which is how it ought to be. Everybody will get laid tonight or wind up dying out in the parking lot, caught in the torrents and foul eddies that have come to claim us all. It's the way it's always been, but now it's even worse.

The animal heads stare down and we look back wondering which of us is the most neglected.

My mother is still here in some fashion, weaving across the wet, stained floor. I don't know whether she's alive or dead, but her presence remains behind. She knows their speech and fears, and she smells no different than any of them. I can feel her nearby, breezing past, just out of eyeshot. The cloying stink of sweet perfume, sweat and recklessness. She was sitting on the stool that I'm sitting on right now when she met my father, or so I've heard.

"You wanna dance, Verbal?" the woman asks. She's creeping towards forty but keeps her voice toddler-pitched, swinging her hips out far enough to clip hedges, and knowing this is a ceremony that cannot ever vary.

Verbal Raynes, master of his own fate, at least as courageous as his cousins and uncles, drags his fingernails across the bar top, digging out thin curling gouts of shellac. He tells her, "Why the goddamn not? Let's go, honey!"

Across the haze sits Betty Lynn, her baby fat almost gone since I last saw her. Her stomach is flat, and at nineteen the harsh eons of experience are alive in her eyes. She tilts her head at me, her teacher in these lessons, as if giving thanks. I nod back.

The wild boar continues its judgment from above. My mother, unseen but only inches away, titters. The smoke circles around us until I can almost believe we no longer exist.

We do, and we know this, but there's no need to ever admit it.

CHANTING, they hurl hexes.

The river is flooding out the bottoms and a host of granny witches, led by Velma Coots, have staked out the house. They're parked there in the woods at the edge of our property, performing rituals and pointing their fingers and curses. It's starting to piss me off just a tad.

I head into the storm and face them. Besides Velma Coots there're six other women—three of them homely, one a beautiful teenager, an elderly hag and an ancient crone. They wear shawls and rags for this ceremony, lace wrapped three times around their hair. In a matter of seconds I'm as drenched as they are. They're all grounded deeper than any tree around us. They've come from out of the swamp for this bizarre meeting—this invocation.

"We need your seed," Velma Coots says.

"Will you cut that shit out, lady!"

"We have to have your vinegar." Water rushes into her mouth as she speaks. I turn and spot Dodi in the bedroom window, rain spouting in a thick stream from the weathervane and arching directly before her. She's excited by the role she's playing in this confrontation. Behind her there's a sudden blur of activity. Stirring shadows as my brothers lurch forward. They understand that they too have a part in this service. Our seed is the same.

I really want a cigarette. "No."

"Your pride is going to cost us all our lives!"

"You say that standing out here in the middle of it?"

"I'm doing what I have to do."

"We all are."

"Not you. You've got a duty to perform, Thomas."

A laugh starts deep in my chest but it doesn't get too far. "There's power in names Dodi said. My name is a part of me and so is my pride. You can't have one without the other."

The tempest moans and tears at us, with the sumac and cottonwoods and willows bowing and waving wildly all around. I won't wind up like my father, and I won't be mocked.

"This storm's a reckoning that's come looking for you, Thomas. They out there, the dead."

"I don't much mind."

"Dodi'll get some of your brothers' seed, if not yours."

"I don't doubt it."

The other conjure women begin a different chant, something with a sing-song lilt and an Assyrian melody. It's a piece of antiquity, this song, and it sounds right on the brunt of the thunder. I tap my foot in the mud, going with it. They spin and thrust their hands in my face. None of them has said a word directly to me.

I ask the teenager, "What's your name?"

She draws back as if I've slapped her. Her nostrils flare as ozone burns and the lightning skips by. Drowned grebes and ducks float by our feet, and the mud laps like whitecapped breakers on an ocean. The Crone looks from me to the girl and goes, "Ssssshhh, chile!" A name has power, and to allow another to know it is a dangerous venture.

The wet lace runs across the girl's forehead while glimmers of sheet lightning ignite to our left, to our right.

"Lottie Mae."

"You work at the mill."

"Yes."

"You ought to be there right now."

She's offended by this small talk and because I've questioned her competence as one of my own employees. Even in the gray soaked day I can see a flush of crimson enter her cheeks. "I got someone to cover my shift. And you shouldn't be caring about such things right at this here moment. You've got a greater responsibility, I hear tell. You've an obligation to Kingdom Come."

"No more than you or anyone else." I gaze at her and she holds my stare. I think I'm falling in love. I take a step forward and she nearly retreats into the brush. "How far would you go?"

"What?"

"For what has to be done."

She catches on quick and freezes in her tracks. "I—"

"What would you do, Lottie Mae? To get my vinegar."

"Listen here, this ain't a—"

I reach for the ends of the lace and unwrap her

face. She's beautiful with a dark tangle of short black hair and defiant eyes. I draw my hand across her throat and watch the red deepen there as she quickly slips away. "Go home, ladies."

Velma Coots stomps towards me about to get into it again. The Crone hovers at her shoulder. "Thomas, you can't hide from this burden. It's a commitment that's come for you."

"That's enough, Velma Coots." The sound of her name brushes her back some. "I'm tired of this. Go home. The storm will end tomorrow."

"The swamp demons don't give up that easy, son. This commotion won't ever stop until you—"

"It's already stopping. Can't you feel it?"

The rain abates and Velma Coots seems a little stunned, her fingers and pink nub waving slightly as if testing the air. It's got her curious but she's still wary.

The other conjure women withdraw from around me now, the Crone drawing signs and wards in the wind. I do have pride, and ego, and I'm not certain if they've just fed it or sucked it clean like the marrow from a cracked chicken leg.

Lottie Mae cocks her chin and looks up at the window. A plethora of hands and arms are moving, in spasms, and wave down to her.

CHAPTER FIVE

I once met a dead boy in the swamp.

I was seven or eight years old and had somehow gotten away from the yard. I heard my mother calling after me, high-pitched but not quite wailing. It was as if she were singing a slow ballad. As I listened I thought I was following the sound of her voice back to the house.

Instead I'd become turned around and continued heading deeper into the broad channels of slough, steering towards the swamp. I wandered for hours over muddy embankments, past cabbage palms and shagbark hickory, hearing her the entire time—or only thinking I heard her—unafraid as I walked on.

Eventually I began climbing through tangles of mangrove and chickasaw plum, at the bank of the river. Tendrils of fog eased over the stagnant morass and pulsed beyond the cypress and fallen ironwood. I wasn't tired. The world had opened up for me in a way it never had before.

I studied the lesson being taught. The voice of my mother had stopped but still I pursued it. That song remained behind in the air like the scent of jasmine. It carried into trees and sparkleberries. I climbed through the shallows and stood hip-deep in the bayou, knowing my place. One of my places, at least.

The boy had been half-buried in mire.

A shovel lay nearby but someone hadn't finished covering him over. His left arm hung at an angle outside of the grave—fist clenched—and his right foot lay bent in such a way I knew the bones had been shattered. The sneaker remained neatly laced up, double-knotted with a looping bow, just like my own.

Most of his face could still be seen. His eyes were open. They were gray and drying.

He was about my age, maybe a year or two younger. I kneeled and confronted the body, wanting to touch it but unwilling to put my hand on his skin. Part of his neck was dirty but the rest was pale and clean as if it had been scrubbed. I could clearly see the dark bruises under his Adam's apple the size and shape of fingerprints.

"Hey, young'n."

For an instant I thought the boy was talking to me. I peered closer. I ran my fingers through his short, blonde hair. His mouth was filled with skimmer dragonflies and mosquitoes.

"Young'n, you there, kid!"

I spun and stared further into the slough until I saw a thread of white smoke rising. A man sat in the morass puffing on a cigarette. He waved amiably and asked, "You wearing a belt, son? Yeah, you are, I can see it from here. I need a belt and a nice strong piece of stick."

He had no shirt on and his body seemed carved of brass. The muscles rippled on his heavy arms and massive chest as he slowly raised the cigarette and puffed deeply. A broken-backed bull gator thrashed in the bog, squirming and rolling, dying. In its jaws was a human leg.

It was the man's. He had used his shirt to try to staunch the flow of blood pouring from the stump, but it hadn't made an effective bandage. He'd knotted the sleeves together but they were wet and loosening. He calmly continued smoking, apparently in no particular hurry to move, even though he was bleeding out.

"I need you belt and a stick so I can make a tourniquet. You do know what a tourniquet is, don't you, boy?"

"Yes," I said.

"That's good, I had a gut-feelin' you was a smart kid. My name is Herbie Ordell Jonstone, come here from Tupelo Mississippi. Don't be scairt none, you could do me a righteous turn, you could."

"Uh huh."

I stared down at the boy and kept stroking his hair.

"That there is my son, Johnny Jonstone. This bull gator here got to him first. A tragedy it is, a man losing his firstborn and his leg like this all on the same afternoon. But you can help to make it right."

"I can?"

"Good Lawd above, yes. We need more heroes like you in this here world, boy, trust me on that. Someone of distinguished valor and admirable exploits, that's what you got a chance to be. Willing to help a man down on his luck and in pressing adversity. I bet this here story receives some national coverage on the tee vee, and folks from all around our great nation will hail your name."

"You really think so?"

"For certain. And tell me now, just what is you name?"

"Thomas."

"You gonna make your mama proud today, Thomas. You're my savior is what you are."

"I know it," I told him, taking my belt off. I stepped over to a loblolly pine and endeavored to break a thick piece of branch off. It took a while of twisting and bending it over with all my weight on top before it to finally came free.

"That's it, Thomas. Now bring it on over here to me. The water ain't but waist-high on you. And don't be scairt of that there bull, he's done in for, that's a fact. He sure did try to even the score though. Hurry it up some, I'm startin' to feel a might dizzy here."

"I'll tell you what, Herbie," I said.

"What's 'at? You'll...?"

I dropped my belt and the loblolly branch on the dead boy's chest. "We'll leave it up to Johnny Jonstone."

He gave a quizzical head ratchet. "The hell you say?"

"If he brings it out to you, then you'll be fine and me and Johnny'll both be men of admirable exploits. He'll make his daddy proud today."

"Hold on now," Herbie said, beginning to seethe. I liked the look on his face. He flicked the butt of his cigarette into the bayou and it bounced off the flailing tail of the dying gator. "I don't believe you quite understand the situation we got goin' on here, boy."

"And I believe I do."

"Thomas, you come on out here now, 'fore I— "

"If Johnny doesn't get up, then I guess you run

out of blood right there where you are and them other gators will come take you away. You hear 'em calling now, don't ya?"

They were roaring in the distance. Herbie turned in the slime to listen. The shock was wearing off and some of the pain and fear had started seeping in.

"Sound fair?"

"You little bastard!" he shrieked.

"That any way to talk to your savior?"

"You come on out here right now, young'n! You—"

"No."

"—come this way so I can *squeeze on you some too!*"

I sat and waited while Herbie shouted and tried to crawl towards me, but killing the boy and the gator and having his leg torn off had taken something out of him. He couldn't do much more than flail in place. I half-expected the child to get up and clamber away crying for his mother.

Occasionally I prodded the kid in the chest while patting his head. Cormorants and ring-neck ducks waddled past and, feeling content and safeguarded, I fell asleep in the shadow of white oaks, listening to Herbie's screams.

When I woke up the bodies were gone and my father stood over me with a terrified look in his eyes. The gators had taken the bodies off, I thought, if they'd ever really been there at all.

I followed my father home, my distinguished valor intact.

But my belt was gone.

PRIVATE eye work is not all flashing .45s, dirty cops and beguiling broads in sunglasses, but at least some of it is. Nick Stiel is already having serious problems. Lily's been working him down to a nub, and the good sex is making him feel guilty whenever he thinks of his dead beloved wife.

Stiel now looks as much like the stereotypical P.I. as Lily appears to be the repressed schoolmarm with molten loins. He's begun to drink and the stench of whiskey wafting from him fills my office. I almost enjoy the smell. His eyes are no longer half-lidded. They're wide and gazing around and it's no longer an ordeal for him to bear witness to life. It may drive him completely insane before the end, but he'll jack-knife over the rim glaring at it all.

The constant assault of her stern glance has pounded upon his fractures and burst him open. He's leaking out between the seams. It's a lot to deal with: Lily's onslaught, that slithering tongue, the ever-loosening bun of her shining hair. The revelations of an exquisite body beneath such ill-fitting clothes, and the alluring mania of her lust. And all the while having Eve stare at him, pigtails bobbing.

His calluses have been scrubbed off, probably with pumice stone. His fingers are as pink as a sow's ass. I can imagine Lily arguing with him about how she prefers smooth hands, spending hours softening his scars with oil and lotion and then scouring them off. They're as fine as velvet now. He's getting a little beer gut and hasn't practiced martial arts since he arrived in Kingdom Come.

Stiel's instincts are still sharp though. I can sense that he's running all the variables around in his head, perplexed in a lot of new ways but no longer distracted by his wife's death. He perceives me as a possible threat and he's much more alert than he was before.

"How goes it?" I ask.

His integrity and honesty mean a great deal to him, and he's not afraid to admit his failure. "I haven't found a damn thing out about either case yet."

It doesn't bother me. I didn't think the report and maps and photos I gave him would ever do much good. His conflicted soul over Lily and Eve has only added to his other burdens. Stiel was pretty much lost from the very beginning, but we all have to play our strings out to the end.

I've heard that he's made friends in Potts County. He enjoys the company of the granny witches, and Abbott Earl has mentioned that Stiel spends a lot of time at the monastery, hoping to get centered again but not having much luck.

"Don't let it nettle your conscience," I say. "You didn't have much to work with right from the start."

"Thanks, but I'm still on it. I'm going to stay in town until it's done."

He frowns, wondering what kind of play I'll make next. There's something of an implicit threat in his voice, as if he's running the show. I toy with the idea of telling him that I won't pay for any more of his time. If he hasn't discovered anything by now, as I suspected he wouldn't, there's not much point in continuing.

But I know it's a matter of pride with him, perhaps the last vestige of self-respect that remains. He wouldn't leave if they ran him out with pitchforks, and I still want to keep somebody close to Eve.

"No luck at all with the dog kicker?"

"Nothing. It's still occurring pretty regularly, despite all the precautions taken by your neighbors. It's clearly somebody who's intimate with your ways and knows your pets."

"Uh huh, it's got to be one of us."

"Yes."

"Have you been keeping in touch with Sheriff Burke?"

"That runt has a nasty disposition and he's dumber than a shrub. He's had no leads and, frankly, I don't think he cares much."

"He never has."

It's time to talk about Eve. Stiel fidgets a bit like a schoolboy waiting outside the principal's office. I wait to see if he'll crack the ice about the girl, but he doesn't.

"Has Eve spoken?" I ask.

"No, she hasn't. But she is capable of speech."

"Oh?"

"In her dreams, she mutters. She's mumbled a few words."

I take a stab. "Anything about a carnival?"

"No. Why?"

I don't answer. I should've kept my mouth shut. I haven't seen Drabs in days and he and Velma Coots have got me on edge. I let out a breath and Stiel inspects the office, the gouges on the desk. He knows Lily's work and a twinge of jealousy flicks through him.

The genuine characters of both Lily and Eve are not that different, I suspect, although I have no idea what they might actually be. I don't have to ask if Lily has bought her clothes more appropriate to an older girl. I'm certain Eve is still wearing the bobby socks and plastic black shoes.

I wonder if she's the child my brothers claim to have murdered, returned now to hold judgment upon us all.

Stiel gets up to leave, gazing about, trying to find evidence. He knows that there's more here than meets his eye. The rosy tips of his fingers must tingle. He wants answers and he's nearly, but not quite, willing to rumble with me to get them. If only I could oblige.

"Stiel?"

He stops without turning to face me.

"Does Eve still have that all-day sucker?" I ask.

The word falls from his lips like black blood coughed up from a chest wound. "Yes."

I wonder if he's slept with little Eve yet, and if so, what it was like. He stares back at me now, already doomed or just about to be. Still, he holds his head high and walks straight and tall. There's no curve to his spine and there's a hint of a smile in those eyes. He's got something to hold onto inside, even if it carries him to hell.

It must be worth the price.

"It's this damn town," he hisses, hand on the knob, as he lets out a soft, angry groan.

"Don't I know it."

REVEREND Clem Bibbler, Drabs' father, asks me to meet him at his church. I arrive just before dark, with the sinking red sunlight igniting the kudzu weed that runs rampant across the small brown crabgrass lawn. He stands in the front doorway, framed by drawn shadows. I stare at the roof.

The moist heat of night claws between my shoulders and sweat pools there. The reverend is dressed in a heavy black suit, as always. He's comfortable and cool no matter how mindless the temperature makes everyone else. Perhaps his faith assuages and soothes him.

He aims his chin at me. The muscles in his glistening black face are taut, cords of his neck well-defined and showing every dark vein. His hands are clasped behind his back. He confronts the world—or only me—with a stoic, impenetrable front. He swallows once and his collar bobs. The reverend doesn't unsettle me but he is perhaps the only man alive who carries any weight in my book. I'm not sure why.

"Thomas," he intones. His voice is low and resounding and echoes across the empty yard.

"Hello, Reverend Bibbler."

He ushers me into the small wood-frame church. Two ropes leading up to the steeple creak and twine in the breeze. The bell sways and there's an almost imperceptible yet constant thrum. Forty years ago this was a one-room schoolhouse where my grandmother taught the children of Kingdom Come. She was discovered dead on the roof, impaled with a reap hook, and the murder goes unsolved today.

I've been in this church a hundred times and hardly ever think of my grandmother skewered to the shingles, but now I'm having a hard time getting past the image. She hung upside down for most of the afternoon, rotting in the sun, until she was discovered by my mother, who'd been sent to search for her. My gaze keeps drifting towards the rafters, to the west wall where strange words were found outside. Reverend Clem Bibbler knows why I'm looking there but he doesn't comment.

The place is extraordinarily clean. His congregation is still afraid that Drabs is going to get naked up there or that the dog kicker will get after their hounds while they're away, so they've been skipping his sermons. If it wears on his nerves, he doesn't show it in the least.

He leads me to the first pew and gestures for me to sit. I don't. He clasps his hands behind his back again and strolls in front to his own pulpit. The cross on the wall is small, plain, and smells of lemon furniture wax.

"Have you seen my son recently, Thomas?"

"No."

"Drabs hasn't been home for several days. I fear for him."

"Don't. He might be cursed but so long as he keeps his clothes on in public he'll be all right."

Reverend Bibbler pulls a face. "Please don't border on blasphemy. I'm greatly worried."

"So am I. I'm sorry to be facetious. I'll see if I can track him down."

"I'd be grateful. Do you have any idea where he might be?"

"No, but if he's still in town, I'll find him."

"Thank you. I appreciate your efforts."

"Of course."

An all-prevailing silence washes over and engulfs us. It always happens. We're at different ends of the earth, he and I, though at times he thinks of me as something of a wayward son, and I feel for him the way I did for my father. I should leave but he has more to tell me, and he's working his way up to saying it. I sit in the pew and give it time.

"Did he tell you that he no longer wishes to preach the Word?"

"Yes."

He expects a lengthier response but I see no point. We've had conversations exactly like this one many times since Drabs married Maggie to me down by the river and he lost himself within the grace of God.

The reverend wants to draw me into a tête-à-tête, but the possibility annoys him all the same. "And what are your thoughts on that?"

"It's his life."

"But admit the truth. You'd prefer if he gave up the pulpit."

"I'd prefer if the pulpit gave him up."

"What you call a curse is special consideration under the Lord."

"I only want him to be happy."

Reverend Bibbler, for all his faith and sermonizing, still believes the damage done to Drabs may only be psychological or neurological. He once asked me for the money to send Drabs down to Atlanta for an MRI scan, which I gave to him. Drabs fell into a fit of tongues inside the small resonance chamber and the doctors, after two days of observation, had him committed to the psychiatric wing. It took a month and four lawyers to get him released.

"I pray for him each morning and night, that he'll find release from his burden. I pray—"

"Maybe you shouldn't."

He gets my meaning immediately but decides to play it out some. "Excuse me, Thomas?"

He speaks my name with a singular flourish. It's the name of the Doubter and he tries to say it the way he thinks Christ would have. All he thinks I need are a few Sundays listening to his preaching in order to get my mind right.

"Maybe you shouldn't pray for him. Drabs needs something else in his life right now. He always has, but especially for the time being. Perhaps you should help him attend to those matters first."

There's more of the Puritan in him than he thinks. He would've been at home in Salem seated beside Cotton Mather, laying stones on Giles Corey's chest and hanging possessed dogs.

"What matters are they?" he asks.

"You're already aware of them."

"He dreams of you often."

"I know, he's told me."

The Reverend is a Christian warrior who wears the highly polished armor of the Lord. Still, he's no fool or instigator, and he knows that he must share his control of Kingdom Come's spiritual well being with other forces. His mama told him stories about the bayou and the deep woods, the same way all our mothers did. The nature of his belief is more emancipated than most, as it has to be in Potts County.

He's also a shrewd reader of souls. "Don't hate my son, Thomas."

"He's my only friend."

"Yes, he is. And he loves you deeply. Remember—"

The pause lengthens as I hang waiting. "What?"

"He's no more a burden to you than you are to him."

MOONLIGHT pours through the willows and swamp cyrilla as I continue to cruise the backroads of town. I keep expecting Drabs to come stumbling out of a drainage ditch, clothed or unclothed, maybe leaping from behind a patch of dogwood scrub. I can only hope I won't find his castrated corpse dangling from a birch limb, swinging slightly in the rising wind.

I drive slowly, circling the highway, surveying all the shanties and ramshackle cabins dappling the hills and hollows. Pinewood boards that don't fit in door frames are held in place with knotty crossbars. Screens hang from broken hinges. Televisions and radios mumble politics and weather and canned laughter from sit-com hijinks. Banjos and drawls float from splintered slats. I head further into the marshland, past Doover's Five & Dime.

I should go to the flat rock. Drabs—or someone—might be waiting there for me, but I'm moving in some vague pattern, following a different course. I tug the steering wheel left and right without reason in mind, riding down routes that are little more than ruts through the woods.

The moon beckons, so what the hell.

I think about Lottie Mae, the teenage granny witch who, presumably, was after my vinegar. We've got something in store for each other, but whether it's going to be worthwhile or just dangerous I've no idea. Maybe she's lying out there on the flat rock right now, nude in the silver blazing of the night, eviscerated or waiting for me to climb onto her. Maybe she's holding a reap hook.

A smear of black motion off the side of the road lunges free. I stomp on the brakes and hang onto the wheel as the truck swerves wildly to the left.

Bursting through the brambles, Betty Lynn rushes in front of the truck and I nearly clip her. The truck goes into a skid and grinds up gravel and mud as I swerve into the weeds. She lays in the dirt, stunned. I get out and check her over in the glare of the headlights to make sure that I haven't hit her. There's no blood but she's covered in sweat, disheveled and confused.

She blinks at me without recognition. Her face and arms are torn up with scratches. She's been running and crawling through the fields and tobacco leaves are mashed into the knees and seat of her jeans.

"They..." she gasps. "They comin'...behind me."

"Who?"

"They started followin'...I heard 'em...ran."

"Who is it, Betty Lynn?"

She still can't pull it together, and she's trembling so hard that she shakes right out of my grip. "Dunno...think they got guns. Heard sounds...coulda been a rifle bolt sliding...mebbe not..."

She can't say any more as she takes in heaving gulps of air. I get her into the truck and turn off the headlights.

I wait, expecting to hear drunken laughter, hoots and hollers. To see a couple of flashlight beams waving back and forth, guys whistling and calling *Here, kitty, kitty*. That sort of crap. A few good ol' boys out having fun chasing after a pretty girl, things getting just a touch out of hand. It happens.

But there's only silence. I light a cigarette, acutely aware of the irony as I lean against the truck on the outskirts of a tobacco field. I look back and Betty Lynn is bewildered and exhausted, staring at me, still sweating. Her hair and clothes are drenched. They must've chased her all the way from Leadbetter's parking lot, almost three miles away.

"Let's go," she says.

"It'll be all right."

"But—"

"Hold on."

"Thomas...."

There is a sound of crackling, and soon I see two distinct orange glows approaching in the brush. They come nearer and nearer, then stop and hover in the distance.

I can't help myself, I burst out laughing.

These fuckers are actually carrying torches.

It's got my curiosity up, that's for certain. My chuckling catches in my throat and sticks there. If they've got guns they haven't used them yet. No smell of gunpowder beneath the burning tallow. No straight-taper twenty-two inch barrels pointing out from between the dogwood leaves. Embers float and rise in the breeze. I take a step towards the brush and the glow recedes. Skittish pricks. I shake my head and toss the cigarette butt.

I talk into the darkness.

"Here, kitty, kitty," I say. "Somebody want to come out and play?"

The flames dip closer together, converge, then separate again.

"Don't be shy now." My voice is full of anger even though I'm not. "You want her, you just need to get past me. You want me, well, there's no obstruction at all then. Let's confer and have a nice colloquy. I'm open to any and all discussion."

They hesitate for another moment, wavering, then begin to back off. I watch the fires recede into blackness.

I get back into the truck and start down the road. Betty Lynn says, "Oh God, no, please don't take me to yer house."

"I won't. I'll drive you back home to your place."

"Mama's gonna kill me, she's 'lergic to tobacco."

"When you spend all night in Leadbetter's you stink

of smoke anyway."

"She don't mind cigarettes, but she worked in the fields most'a her life and she hates the reek of it."

We drive on. She takes my hand and holds on to it tightly, then draws it into her lap. The one time we've made love started out with a similar display before we crept into the back seat. After a minute or so she begins to weep softly, but that passes by pretty fast. I keep clean rags from torn up T-shirts in the glove box. She knows it because it's also where I keep the condoms. She grabs a couple of the scraps and wipes her face, arms and neck down.

"Thomas, the baby...."

"Yes?"

"It wasn't yers. It was Jasper Kroll's, from down at the mill, but I—"

"Don't worry about that."

"I'm sorry I lied."

"It doesn't matter."

I drop her off and swing around past the railroad tracks. I park on them looking forward into the hills and back into the swamp, as the moon boils down over Kingdom Come.

I wonder if those torch-bearers have captured and lynched Drabs.

Worse, I can't help wondering if he was one of them.

IN my mother's dreams she stands in front of the school staring up at her own murdered mother hanging across the peak of the roof. My mother—the girl— is eleven years old. Blonde curls drape across the shoulders of her gingham dress. She's a tomboy and her elbows are scraped. Dust devils whirl past her knees and the dull roar of wind plays in the top branches of the cottonwood trees.

The girl gapes but is not frightened. She feels only a wrenching, unformed sadness that collects in her chest. She knows her mother is dead, butchered, laid out on view although there's no one else to see this. The reap hook catches a glint of light that winks back at her. She steps closer to the school, which has a thin but drying stream of blood oozing down across the west wall.

The air smells foul and fishy. Potts County has been suffering under a drought for the entire summer and the river has dropped almost two feet. Fish, beaver and possum lay putrefied on sandbars, and the bottoms reek with dankness. The wind is blowing in the fetor, which coats the area like a funnel of smoke.

Someone has been here recently, not just to kill her mother in such a bizarre, vicious fashion, but also to write with her blood across the white clapboard. For some reason both sights are distinct and separate in her mind. These are independent, detached, possibly unconnected displays of outrage.

The dead mother up there on the roof, the writing here on the wall.

The words are in a precise and deliberate block lettering, but appear strangely stylish. The girl presses closer and realizes they've been written with a piece of chalk, which lays red-tipped in the dust. It has been run through the blood so that the letters are white at the center and crimson at the edge, where the blood has thinned around the dense chalk marks and then run off. They are, in fact, rather pretty.

DO NOT CONSIDER THIS ANOTHER DE-
FEAT. FORGIVE THE SHORTCOMINGS. GRAV-
ITY. LOVE IS ONLY LUST DRESSED UP FOR
CHURCH. PENETRATION. GRAVY. MEANING.
SIGNIFICANCE. THE HAM IS ON THE TABLE.

These words are only a little higher than her own
eye-level, perhaps proving that the killer—or at least
the writer—is only slightly taller than she is herself.
She doesn't understand or care for these declarations
and washes them off, standing on a stool used by her
classmates when being graded on oral reports. She is
responsible for washing the blackboard at the end of
class every day and she does a good job. However,
when the wall dries the words seep through again. Her
father and the sheriff are angry with her for disturbing evidence.

The reap hook can't be traced. It could belong to
anyone in Potts County, including the sheriff, including her father. The summer heat and drought make
matters much worse. A white woman's murder can't
go by without some retribution being served up. Over
the next month four colored folks are lynched and six
houses burned down into the dust.

The killer and the writer are never found. No one
is ever found in Kingdom Come even though some
are lost day after day.

In my mother's dreams the ham is on the table.

CHAPTER SIX

I spend a few days with the Holy Order of Flying Walendas, riding the donkey, baking bread at dawn. Abbott Earl is eager to speak with me, but it's not yet sixth hour and we're committed to our vow of silence.

Seekers of every variety wander the grounds, searching out God, themselves, their pipe dreams and their sins. They seem to enjoy the bread though, and a certain amount of pride fills me. The trick is to knead the dough for at least twenty minutes, until your wrists begin to ache, before placing it into the oven. And raisins, use lots of raisins.

More pilgrims, acolytes, alcoholics and the insane arrive every day. Some are irritated and bitter, some driven by their fears and nameless needs. They wear the cowls hoping to lose their desires within the depth of shapeless robes, but that almost never happens. They walk the wire across the chasms of their own souls, looking down into the great depths as, step by step, they cross to the distant side. On occasion they've learned something by the time they get there, but not always, and usually not what they expect.

Each to his own method. They run naked in the

woods or recite the same prayer two thousand times while tapping little gongs before them. Or they howl from the abbey rooftop or cut the heads off of chickens and paint the ground with bloody symbols that appear more childish than Satanic. The penitents strip the skin off their backs with cat-o-nine-tails that have jagged pottery shards tied to the leather. They flay themselves so they might one day be covered in fleece. Meditation can be like murder for some of them.

At sixth hour Abbott Earl finds me. He's still got the hard muscles from when he drove a bulldozer and worked to drain the swamp. I keep the dollar he paid me for the old hospital in my wallet, and I take it out every now and again and think about how that single pack of bandages in the abandoned building saved his life. I glance around wondering what might save my life if I ever needed it—the raisins I use in the bread, these thistles in my robes, or over there, that pile of donkey shit. Perhaps they all have their place in God's plan.

He says, "I need to speak with you, Thomas."

"I'm listening."

"I'm not sure how important this may be but I felt that I should broach the subject with you. It concerns Sister Lucretia."

"Lucretia Murteen."

That's the one-eyed woman he was bedding down with a few years back while drowning in tequila, after he'd grown as lost as my father over the failed project to clear the jungle and bring in strip malls. When he found his faith she did as well and became a nun in the order, a bride of the Flying Walendas. I've seen her in the monastery tending the gardens mostly, keeping to herself.

"What about her?"

"You know that she and I were once intimate. Before we started the order. Back when—"

"You've got nothing to be ashamed about."

"And I'm not, to be sure. But it's also true that she's been acting…reticent lately. Perhaps a bit taciturn. She's refuses to tell me what's bothering her. I'm afraid that these troubles are actually making her consider leaving us."

"That's her right."

He waves a hand in the air. "Of course, and normally I'd simply wish her well if that were her decision. We've all got our own courses to follow, wherever they may lead us. I wouldn't dare to interfere so long as she chooses to go willingly and not because she feels she's being forced to do so."

"Forced?"

"Either by this burden or because of someone else here."

"You think one of the monks or travelers has been bothering her? Threatening her?"

"Not as such," he says. "But perhaps she does feel threatened nonetheless. She is a complex woman who's had a lot to bear in her life."

"Why tell me?"

The vertical scars at his wrist are bright in the late afternoon sun as he steeples his fingers under his chin. He nods, thinking things through first before relating anything on to me. "She has…a secret."

I want to say *Not anymore* but manage to restrain myself. "I see."

He taps his incisors together in a nervous tic, eyes beginning to roam. A trickle of blood trails down his neck from where a barb had plucked his skin. "I overheard her praying. She mentioned a name."

"Mine?"

"No. Your brother's. Sebastian."

At the sound of it my side begins to hurt. His teeth marks are still on me where the face had once been. The bite scars are no longer red. They've cooled to a dull gray. A dentist could take an impression and make a good set of dentures.

"Anything specific?"

"No, but I admit that it bothers me greatly."

"Me too."

We stand beneath the darkening sky looking at one another and not getting anywhere fast. I'm not sure what he expects me to do but I'm glad that he came to me. I turn it over for a while trying not to brood, wondering why Lucretia Murteen might mention my brother's name. I head off.

"Where are you going?" Abbot Earl asks.

"To ride the jackass."

SISTER Lucretia Murteen wears a white eye patch that catches the moonlight and spills it at her feet.

She isn't quite dancing but she's more than swaying as she moves across the floor of the empty nursery. She mimes being an R.N. checking on the preemie babies in their incubators. These are precise, fixed actions: turning on the monitors, scrutinizing the tubes and examining the oxygen flow. The controls are delicate.

She reaches into nonexistent cribs, coos and picks up newborns that aren't there—phantoms, perhaps memories. She sits in a rocking chair and rocks the infants as they sleep, carefully inspecting their tiny mittens and woolen beanie hats. There is no rocking chair and I'm shocked at how well she can perform the movement, in that hideous position, tottering to and fro in a seat that's not even under her. Her legs and back must be ready to collapse.

This isn't a selfish endeavor or dream. She walks down the hall and hands the newborns to their spectral mothers in the maternity ward. She sits talking with them for a time, discussing the beautiful infants, their bright and open futures. I can almost hear the mothers sobbing with joy, kissing the tiny foreheads of children whose eyes haven't yet opened.

Sister Lucretia thanks the holy name of Flying Walenda and walks her own wire of conscience. We all do. She stares out the window up at the stars and moves her patch over her good eye.

Moonlight fills her empty socket until it runs into her mouth.

Her teeth glow in the night as she turns blindly to face me, arms wide.

SWEAT dribbles to the kitchen floor. Dodi and Sarah, the two women of the house, face off like ancient enemies watching each other across desert wastes. They're in the kitchen, equidistant from the knife drawer. This has been a battleground for much longer than they've been in the house, and the ghosts in the walls and closets are proof that all it takes to go to war is a matter of time.

Sarah's parents have been mailing long letters to her, begging her to come back home and resume her life as a film student. They offer to pay for graduate school, a new apartment overlooking Central Park, a therapist in Mid-town, whatever it is she might need. I can see by the phone bill that she calls them often, but their conversations usually last for less than five minutes. They no more understand her than she understands herself lately.

Fred has been sending letters too, written on yellow stationary, college-ruled. His penmanship is excessively large and he only writes on every other line. He's in rehab, doing well, clean for nineteen days now, and preparing to film a documentary on addiction.

He's in with two famous rappers, a mediocre actress from a prime time courtroom drama, the grandson of the guy who invented Tater Tots, and a NASCAR driver who hit the fence and took out three bleachers of fans in his last race. After the guy gets clean he'll be formally brought up on manslaughter charges and he's eager to talk about his troubles.

Fred already has six tapes of the driver's confessions on video. Fred's arm is healing okay though it annoys him on rainy afternoons. He hopes she's doing well with the retards. He still wants to be friends and have coffee someday, maybe discuss a few of the older projects that they shelved.

So far as I know, Sarah hasn't written him back yet.

Dodi glares and clicks her fingernails together like castanets. There's a nice salsa rhythm there that almost gets my foot tapping. She and Sarah eye one another with death on the plate. They've shared their beds, but when it comes to my brothers there's no longer enough room for everybody. The tension has been building for weeks now and it's about to snap.

This isn't mere possessiveness. This is desperation. This is a hunger for what the future may bring— love, acceptance, wealth, poetry, maybe even the fate of Potts County. Dodi is still under orders from her mother to keep an eye on me. I've been expecting her to move out, but she remains, night after night, a helpmeet for my brothers.

Jonah defies Dodi's advances. He won't let her give him a sponge bath or feed him or help to brush his teeth anymore. Sarah aids him when she can get by Dodi's defenses. He keeps the three mouths of my brothers going at all hours with the wooing of Sarah. His sonnets have poorly stressed syllables but the meaning is worthy. He has talents that would have meant something a century ago.

His hands, which are the softest of any of ours, can touch her in the right way, delicately brushing her flesh like the advent of a fall leaf. It takes a real passion. Sarah still doesn't join them in bed. She hovers and lingers and abides.

Theirs is a classic structure of tragedy in the making. Dodi floats back and forth between sleeping with me, my brothers, or alone in one of the other bedrooms. There are invisible lines drawn all over the halls, places that cannot be crossed, entered, or left. Sarah is often seated on the floor, her head settled against the base of the foot board. A Midtown shrink would be expensive as hell but maybe he could help.

She purrs while Dodi growls. Jonah whispers while Sebastian spits his malice. Cole seeks only to love, his voice is only love, and Sarah and Dodi should both love him, but of course they hate his guts.

Dodi's breath still smells of bourbon and chocolate, although I haven't bought bourbon for weeks now. She says, "It's time that Yankee up and left."

"Why?" I ask.

"You already know why. Only one woman can rule

any roost and that woman's me. She's gettin' in the way. I got my duty and I don't shirk none'a my responsibilities no matter what."

Sarah is losing the high lilt of a Jewish American Princess and says, "You don't know anything about this place, you little backwater swamp tramp."

"You shut yer mouth!"

"You're only here because your mother gave you up and you've nowhere left to go. Now there's the truth, and that's not enough of a reason for you to still be here. I belong here because I'm willing to stay."

"Are you?" I ask.

"Yes."

"Why?"

Sarah doesn't answer.

This is my house, my home, my space and my family, but none of what's going on concerns me really, and they all know it. Sebastian is eager for a bloodletting. From the bed upstairs he urges the girls to fight so that a hierarchy can once again be established. The bitterness in his voice is so powerful that it spooks a murder of crows out of a tree in the back yard.

Cole tries to calm everyone with reassuring words, but Dodi is gaining a few steps on the knife drawer. Jonah speaks his poetry, also attempting to elicit calm. "*At the egress of your repentance, there, with yet a different sentiment swirling about in your hair, I hear the separate winnows of your beating in time to my heated afterthought. You cry, I weep, and at the heights of our sacred crusades, we drift, we slumber, and at last we sleep.*"

Sarah enjoys listening to his words and is spurred on by his sensibilities. I see now that the faded tattoo on her hip is of the masks of Comedy and Tragedy. She wears her blouse tied at the midriff exactly like

Dodi, but Sarah wears jewelry, a touch of makeup, Christian Dior undergarments. The slight scar around her pierced belly button is hauntingly pale set against her deepening tan.

I inch closer hoping nobody decides to go under the cupboard for a meat cleaver. The windows rattle while Dodi begins a slow smile. She's going to make a jump soon. Sarah still seems a little lost without the coke and Fred and her film, but she's always enjoyed distractions, and this whole thing—us—is just another diversion.

The three throats wail in Sebastian's voice, raving in his wrath, underscored with stanzas dedicated to longing and rapture. Each third of that immense brain wanting nothing else but out.

Jonah continues with his love song. Sarah and Dodi circle each other. I step between them.

My brothers breathe each other's stale breath.

They writhe up there in the darkness while we writhe down here in the light.

MAGGIE is on the other side of the river, sitting in the tall grass with an orchid in her hair. This is about the spot where Drabs married us before being taken by the tongues. I distinctly remember how, even as a nine-year-old boy, my heart slammed in my chest and how it hurt to look into her beautiful face. Some lessons we learn too early for our own good.

Even children shouldn't play these sorts of games under the eyes of God. Maggie kept smiling and looking at me then, just as she does now. Our hands were twined together with wildflower vines, a quaint touch that Drabs despised but Maggie insisted upon.

The bible lay on the shore where he'd dropped it before thrashing out of sight. The water lapped across the sunlight and Maggie stepped closer. God had something to say to us and she tilted her head up as if listening. I brushed the freckles of her throat with my knuckles, which left white impressions upon her sunburned skin. Pages of the bible flapped in the breeze, as though someone unseen were searching for a particular passage and couldn't find it.

The pages stopped whirling, rested open for a moment, and then began to flutter again.

I didn't kiss her because I didn't know how to kiss. I had never played doctor. I started to tell her that I wasn't sure what to do next when she rammed her hot tongue into my mouth and halfway down my throat.

She fell on me in the blazing sun as Drabs caterwauled from somewhere far down the muddy banks.

Now I stand and stare at her as the clouds toss shadows against her legs. She gazes steadily at me, urging me to cross the water. It's only thigh-high at this point, spanning forty feet.

If Drabs was one of the torch-bearers chasing Betty Lynn through the tobacco fields, it only makes sense to me that Maggie was the other. I search for resentment and jealousy in her eyes and find none.

The orchid in her hair is azure tipped in black. She plucks it loose and tosses it in the water, where it spins and trails slowly downstream. She sits with her arms folded over her knees, chin resting on her hands.

My father used to take hundreds of photos of her posed like that and in many other ways—picking apples, swimming, seated in the old tire swing, riding ponies, looming in the willows.

Perhaps he knew that she, like himself, was becoming more of a ghost every day.

I'M surprised to see Lottie Mae, the conjure girl, in
Leadbetter's having a vodka gimlet. She's wearing a
black leather skirt, charcoal blouse and tiny white lace
gloves, the kind that were popular twenty years ago
on the dance club circuit. She's lovely but looks lost
in place and time, like a child dressed for a make-be-
lieve tea party.

Not only is she underage but I didn't think the bartender could make a gimlet to save his soul. She holds
the glass up to the light, turning it first one way and
then the other, relishing the colored light coming
through the thick liquid. She sits alone at one end of
the bar, with maybe twenty guys packed into the other
side. She scares them. The taint of Velma Coots and
the Crone is upon her.

I watch Lottie Mae. The animal heads watch her
too. The guys are quiet, keeping their beer in hand,
maybe a little paranoid. When she glances over, they
turn away in all directions.

I step up, sit beside her, and order two more vodka
gimlets. I haven't had one in years and can't recall
whether I like them or not. The bartender takes the
fifty I've laid out, staying at arm's length and acting as
if the bill might chew through his hand. He breaks it
and puts my change back so close to his side of the
bar that most of it falls behind it, at his feet.

Now he's got to bend over and Lottie Mae and I
will be out of eyeshot above him. He's thinking about
me reaching over and grabbing his throat, shoving a
twizzler in his eye. He's gasping for air just imagining
it. He backs off and gets more money out of the till,

places that in front of me instead. I'm so entertained by his clumsy ballet of terror that I shove the change back at him for a tip, but he's already at the other end of the bar with the rest of the guys.

I take a sip and can't completely stifle a groan. Lottie Mae chuckles even though she hasn't even looked at me so far. I wonder what her mission is tonight and whether I'm to be any part of it.

Her short dark hair is styled into little feathered points. The last time I saw her, in the storm of souls, we were both soaked and steaming. Now, without the drama of the lightning and the tragedy of the granny witches' chanting, we can face the turning of the wheel.

Another laugh flits from her throat and I suddenly realize that she's drunk out of her mind.

"Lottie Mae?"

"You asked me what I was prepared to do. Tha's what you asked." She's slurring her words so badly they run into one another. She exhales everything at once, and it all smells as if it's been inside her a long time. "Well, here it is, the answer you've been waiting on. I'm ready for you now."

"Forget it." She shakes as if laughing, shoulders rolling, but nothing comes out. "Can't do that."

"I think you can."

"No no, it ain't right, listen to me, you gotta listen—"

"You haven't been to the mill."

She slumps in her seat, rouses for an instant, then sags again. I keep my hand on her lower back so she won't topple over. She relaxes and leans against me, blinks a few times trying to get through the fog. "I quit your ole mill. You don't own me, I go where I want. Don't you bother me none 'bout that."

"I promise I won't."

"Well all right."

I shove the vodka gimlet away but the bartender won't come over and let me have something else. The men speak in hushed tones, playing darts and trying to keep watch of us. They can't hit a damn thing on the board and the solid thunk of the dart points nailing wood keeps snapping Lottie Mae up high in her chair.

"Where are you working now?" I ask.

It takes a second for the question to register. "Doover's Five & Dime. Order me another one of these. I want another one of these, before the road."

"You've had too much to drink."

"Have not."

"You're going to be ill."

"Am not." She draws back and eyes me as if seeing me for the first time. A moan fills her chest and quickly dies out as if she's lost her breath. I enjoy the weight of her small body against my hand and rub her back gently. She sticks out a forefinger and tries to tap me in my chest but misses by six inches. "You think I'm afraid, don't you."

"No."

"Yes, you do, I can tell. You're so goddamn smug, aren't you. Sitting there like you're emperor of Potts County. Well, I'm not scared of you. And I'm not scared of doing it either, if that's what you're thinking. I've done it plenty of times. So you just come along."

"Where?"

That thwarts her and she frowns. The aftertaste of vodka is starting to work its way back up her throat and she keeps scowling, scraping her teeth across her tongue. "I don't know. I'll think of something. I don't want to go home to do it. Oh wait, your truck. I heard you got a truck. Do you have a truck?"

"Yes."

The glow of triumph lights her face. She looks like a little girl who's just unwrapped her favorite Christmas present. This might be good for my ego if it didn't make me feel like such an imbecile. "Ah, they was right, come on then."

"No."

"But I'm all set." She takes another sip of her drink and she's got a death-grip on her glass. "You wanted to know, and now you know."

"Yes, now I know."

"I'm ready."

She tries sliding off the chair but I hold her in place. "No, Lottie Mae, you're not."

"Am too, I say. Don't you want me?"

"I—"

Her lips quiver as she begins to snicker. It's a harsh noise made even uglier by the fact that she's on the verge of crying. "I know you want me."

"I like the gloves," I tell her. "They're a nice touch."

"You making fun of me, you sonuvabitch?"

"No."

"Let's just get it over with." Lottie Mae stirs and raises her head some but can't focus on me anymore. The darts striking the wall make her buck as if she's being stabbed. She manages to wheel away from me and I know she's going to fall off her chair and be sick. I catch her as she drops over backward still holding tightly to her glass. Liquor spills onto her lap and she flinches and lets out a soft noise. It's partly a sigh but mostly an infant's grunt of dissatisfaction.

We barely get outside into the parking lot in time.

She heaves in the middle of the gravel walkway just as a couple of bikers are striding up. I rub the back of her neck and make soothing sounds the way I did when my mother first started going out and drinking, hiding bottles all over the house.

I don't know what the hell she had for supper but it comes out raw, mean, and bloody-looking. The granny witches could probably read signs in the spatters of bile but it's all just a mess to me. She goes to wipe her mouth with the back of her hand but notices she's wearing the gloves. She doesn't want to ruin them and holds her hands up and flutters her fingers, groaning and sobbing now. I grip Lottie Mae under her shoulders and drag her to the bushes where she continues retching.

An open hand slaps me hard in the middle of my back.

The biker is six inches taller than me and much wider. He isn't a body builder but he's moved some steel or stone in his time. He wears heavy motorcycle boots, a faded red T-shirt with the sleeves cut off, and black jeans frayed at his ankles. He has a small knife concealed in his belt buckle, the kind you pull like an old beer can tab. There are poorly done prison tattoos all over his huge arms that remind me of Sarah's masks of Comedy and Tragedy.

One of his biceps reads DARR, which is either a misspelling, an acronym, or his name. He has a shaved head except for three thin, smooth stripes of hair, one on each side and another down the middle.

The other biker—short, slender but well-built—is entranced by Lottie Mae's vomit and kneels over the puddle, grimacing and pursing his lips.

Darr asks me, "Are you planning on doing anything unsavory?"

"Not at the moment," I tell him.

"She's underage."

"Yes."

"And I think she ought to come along with us."

That stops me for a second, and now I've got to look at him a bit differently. "Why's that?"

"A young girl could get badly hurt in just these sort of circumstances, being she's so muddled in a place such as this."

I've got to agree with him. "You're right, but outside of an upset stomach and tomorrow's hangover, she'll be fine."

"I'll take her on home then."

I settle back some trying to get a bead on Darr. I find it odd that if he knows Lottie Mae, he doesn't speak directly to her. True, she's throwing up, but still, he could make some sort of an attempt.

He acts like he's defending her virtue, a knight of the realm. Maybe that's just posturing on his part or maybe he's just hoping to steal off a drunk beauty without too much of a hassle.

None of it quite adds up. I'm pretty certain the bikers aren't headed for the monastery. They don't have the stale air of belief, theological pursuit, or world-weariness about them. But it's clear they've got their own objectives. I look over at the small guy who's still inspecting the splashes.

Darr crosses his arms over his burly chest and takes a deep breath to inflate himself.

"She's my responsibility," I tell him. "I'll make sure that she gets home safely."

"Somehow I tend to doubt that," he says.

We're both getting itchy standing there talking when we really want something to happen. "It's good you're a man who can express his views succinctly. Thanks for the colloquy. Enjoy your night."

I give him my back again. If any action is going to go down, now's the time.

Right on cue his massive fist comes from down low near his knees, aiming for my kidneys. I roll with it, turn aside, and he's so hyperextended with the looping punch that he nearly tips over. He's tough but awkward, and I still can't get past the feeling that all of this has been coordinated for some reason I can't figure out.

I say, "Okay, let's see where this gets us."

He throws a stiff left that I slip but he's already following up with a right cross that catches me on the hinge of my jaw. It's a bad place to get hit, in that nerve cluster. Pain flashes up my face and showers my vision with fiery blots. I dodge and he makes another pass with the left, which taps my temple.

I go low and he thinks I'm reaching in to grab his nuts. He blocks his groin while I yank the blade out of his belt buckle and bring it up to his forehead. Directly at the start of his middle stripe of hair I give a little slash, and the blood immediately begins pouring down his forehead and into his eyes.

The other biker comes over and tells me, "I'm Lottie Mae's brother."

I believe him. He passes by me without another word, takes her gently around her waist and holds her in his arms.

She coughs and sputters. "Clay, I screwed it all up. I was ready. He didn't want me. I tried. I'm sorry."

"You gotta stay away from them crazy old women and their ways, Lottie Mae."

"Them's our ways too."

"No more."

He gets her onto his Harley, where she leans forward heavily against his back. In a few seconds they're gone. Darr keeps bleeding and shambling all over the place, growling and blindly lashing out for me. I take him by the wrist and lead him inside. There's a first aid kit near the phone. I put a butterfly Band-Aid on him and head home, still tasting that goddamn vodka gimlet.

GLOWERING, Velma Coots sits on a sycamore stump outside her shack, one-eyed newts springing around her feet, wingless bats flopping. She holds the short curved blade tightly in her fist. I can hear the sloshing of the black liquids in her brass cauldron from here, spitting.

"You come to make things right?" she asks.

"That depends on whether you're still on that vinegar kick."

"Don't mock, chile. That's what makes the magic work best."

"So you've said. But the storm's over."

She sneers, shakes her head and makes little "feh" noises that might be derisive laughter. "That's what you been thinkin'. But if you believed it you wouldn't be here again. The dead ain't at rest and they got plenty of mischief to make. Evil's still on the lookout."

"Of course it is."

"Well, at least you ain't completely stupid about

that."

"No," I say, "not completely."

"The ghosts are comin'. They in the air. Can't stop them none without some offerings."

We enjoy the evening like that for a while. I smoke a couple of cigarettes and watch the stars appear in the roiling purple sky of the east. Finally, she gets up and leads me into her shack where I sit in a rickety ladder-back chair. There are no flames in the fireplace, just red-hot embers that boil her potions.

She offers me a jug of moonshine and I take a tap that slams down my throat like a runaway freight. I should be going into a coughing fit but my gag reflex has completely seized up. Tears leak onto my cheeks and Velma Coots says, "Made it myself. Smooth ain't it?"

"Gah!"

"Feh. I thought you'd like it."

I haven't had shine in a while and can already feel the enamel on my teeth beginning to peel. The black liquids splash onto the hot stone and sizzle and pop. The reek of flesh and fish strengthens for an instant and then subsides.

I wonder if it's the same stew that I poured my blood into or if this is a new batch. Maybe Dodi's handed off some of my brothers' vinegar and we're in a whole new world of sacrifice. Bats jerk and squirm through the doorway and broadhead skinks bound across the floor. She's still gripping the knife tightly and I'm wary that she might lunge at my neck any second.

"You got a house full of hurt," she says.

"Everybody does."

"Not like you."

That's true, and I start to tell her that I'm thinking of sending Dodi back home to her, but I decide not to. I don't want to go back to changing my brothers' bedpans and feeding their angry slavering mouths and sponging their tangled smelly bodies. Dodi has become a necessity in our home, which is what Velma Coots had been counting on. That's all right, I think, we'll work with it.

"Have you seen Drabs Bibbler?" I ask.

"That poor boy's got special consideration under God."

"I realize that."

"He's earned the right to go his separate way, if he chooses. Don't you go chasing him none."

"He's my friend."

"You sure about that?" she says.

"Yes. Maybe he needs my help."

"Time for that's long gone, I s'pect."

There's almost a judgmental tone in her voice, like she's angry I ever got in his way. Some folks think I should've just let him grow up and marry Maggie, the girl he loved more than anything in this life. I can understand that.

"Tell me about the carnival," I say.

It's the first time Velma Coots refuses to meet my gaze. Something very much like alarm scurries over her face for a moment and is gone. She scratches the tip of her nose and runs her tongue over her remaining few teeth. I hand her the jug of shine back and she takes a long pull that could blind seven men. Now we're getting somewhere.

"It's not my place to talk about that."

"I need to know. It was the last thing that Drabs said to me before he vanished. I promised his father that I'd find him, but so far I haven't had any luck. I think he's hiding from me."

"Why's that, you reckon? That boy's got the good Lord on his side so he surely ain't scared of you none. And you ain't afraid of him or any storm. So far as I see you ain't a'fearing it for nobody else either."

"It might have something to do with my parents."

"Well now, it just might at that."

She puts the jug down at her feet and I notice her hand is bandaged. She's taken off the tip of her other pinkie.

"Christ, lady, quit doing that to yourself!"

"Someone's got to make up for the sacrifices you ain't offering."

I try not to let out a sigh but it still hisses between my teeth. I take a step forward and the light of the embers rises and falls against the ceiling. "You act like I need to make amends."

"That's right. You owe a debt."

"To who?" I ask. "For what?"

"You don't really care. You ain't here for me nor the town nor Drabs Bibbler neither. I know what you got on your mind, Thomas. Now you listen here good. You leave that girl alone."

The taste of moonshine has given me a thirst I can't shake. I grab up the jug and take another sip, and this time it hits the good place. "You're the one who brought her into this. You brought her to my house."

"She come to help, and help she did."

"You used her and you're still using her. Stop sending teenage girls around to seduce me."

"That what she done, huh? That what my Dodi done? Them jezebels beguiled an innocent boy like you?"

"Velma—"

"They know their duty to Kingdom Come and its people. It's you who's shirking your load."

"There's a geek at the carnival."

"There usually is."

"He wants to talk with me."

"Yes, I do believe. The signs say so."

There's a knock from under the floor. Maybe it's rotting boards giving way or maybe it's the murdered up to their mischief. "Who is he, this guy who eats snakes, and what's he want to say?"

The oily shine of pity swims through her eyes. "You'll find that out on your own soon enough."

CHAPTER SEVEN

THAT dead kid is walking around the back yard. His mouth's still full of skimmer dragonflies and mosquitoes that froth from his lips. He's trying to say something, stumbling across the lawn, maybe skipping. He waves and I head downstairs to meet with him.

I turn the corner into the kitchen and a dark tri-fold, predatory figure descends across my way.

It's cold down here. Gooseflesh rises along the backs of my arms and legs, my shoulders, my ass. I step back, aware that I'm naked and curiously embarrassed by the fact. Limbs flail about. They move in the darkness in a fashion that I've never seen before. I reach for the light switch and one of them grabs my wrist tightly, with much more strength than I could've believed. I let out a groan and the grip slackens until I can pull free.

With three mouths, in one voice, Sebastian says, "He isn't dead."

"The kid?" I ask. "I saw him in the swamp and his throat was crushed."

"Not him. I'm talking about the other one."

"What other one?"

"*The man*." Sebastian sighs, the breath from three sets of lungs puffing powerfully against my chest. "The man with one leg. He's back and he wants to put the squeeze on you."

"He'll have to get in line."

"This is serious, Thomas."

I'm taken aback. My brothers have never spoken my name, and it sounds foreign yet familiar coming from those throats. I can still see them moving in the shadows, no longer in spasms, and I ease myself against the far wall. "A demented prick like that only goes after children."

The corpse of the boy is at the back door gesturing me to come outside. Johnny Jonstone wants to take me on a visit to his one-legged daddy. Milkweed bugs cover his shirt, crawling across that horribly bruised neck. Herbie's black fingerprints can still clearly be seen. I've got a powerful urge to follow him through the cypress and titi bushes and hear what he has to say. If indeed he can say anything at all with a crushed trachea, and furthermore being dead.

He taps at the screen door.

Cole says, "Thomas, stay out of the yard tonight."

"Why?"

"Stop asking so many foolish questions and just trust us."

"Do you really expect me to be able to do that?"

"You have to."

Moonlight streams in through the doorway and the kid is silhouetted there, outlined in flaming silver. The insects cling to the screen. When he knocks they fall in clusters at his feet.

"I'm getting tired of so many folks telling me what

I have to do."

"Stop whining," Sebastian adds. "It isn't easy try-ing to reach you this way."

"What does that mean?"

Jonah is still focused on Sarah, who's asleep up-stairs in bed, alone, perhaps even hoping for him. I can hear it in his voice though he tries to stay cen-tered. "You left the back yard once and wound up deep in the swamp. The same thing will happen tonight but you won't be as lucky as you were then. You're not safe."

"Why?"

"You're no longer being guarded."

"But why? Because I didn't hand over my vinegar?"

"Don't be such an idiot."

Silver seeping against my toes, Johnny really kicks up a fuss, stomping on the welcome mat. I walk over. He smiles with teeth covered in dragonflies and scratches harder. His nails are torn but of course there's no blood. Mosquitoes cloud in front of his weathered face. I check for Maggie but she's not un-der the willows. She's given up her watch. No won-der I'm unprotected.

"If you've got anything to tell me, Johnny, you can say it from there."

He shakes his head and beckons me.

Symbolism is strong even when you're walking in your sleep. I keep looking around expecting my par-ents to show up, my mother scampering on the ceil-ing, my father halfway through the wall.

I turn to Sebastian and ask, "Why did Lucretia Murteen mention your name?"

"She didn't."

"But—"

"It's also the name of one of the guys crashing at the monastery. They went at it a couple of times and now she's afraid she's pregnant."

"Oh."

I awaken and I'm standing naked by the window. Dodi is in my bed wrapped in twisted blankets but I don't think we've made love. My brothers sleep deeply, two of them snoring heavily. Sarah's seated on the floor, a sheet draped over her shoulder, watching me.

THE foreman, Paul, comes up to my office to tell me that Lily and the little girl are here to see me. His eyes are spinning and the vertigo has gotten hold of him again. I give him a paper cup full of water to drink until he feels well enough to traverse the stairs once more.

I say, "Thank you, Paul," and he looks at me with a mixture of envy and disdain. I really throw off his day when I show up at the mill.

Lily's carrying a bulging picnic basket, the top flaps angled open to reveal a bottle of wine, wildflowers, corn on the cob.

"I hope we haven't come at a bad time," she says, "But I thought we might have something of a picnic lunch with you."

"That would be lovely," I say. "Hello, Eve."

The girl silently watches me, holding but not licking the all-day sucker. Her sensuality is even more greatly exaggerated now than the first time I saw her. From second to second I'm forced to alter my guess about her age. One moment she might be fourteen, a minute later she's nineteen at least. It keeps me rubbing my eyes and trying to do things with my hands.

No wonder Nick Stiel is unraveling on his way to hell.

Eve goes to the window and looks down at the factory workers below us, holding the sucker before her like a scepter, her other fist firmly planted on her hip. Some of the men on the floor look up and murmur among themselves. She's still wearing bobby socks and tiny plastic black shoes, with her hair in pigtails. She's no longer wide-eyed or confused but instead appears to have a strategy of some kind, anticipating the right moment to implement it. I wonder what Velma Coots might see in the girl that I'm unable to see.

The line slows down immediately and the machinery begins to stall. Nobody can concentrate on the task before them with her blazing eyes glaring down at them. The guys are really coming unstrung and the women start asking questions. I hope to Christ that nobody sticks a hand too far into the belts. Paul's got to be about ready to throw a fit. He calls lunch a half hour early and shuts down the line. I make a note to give him a bonus.

Lily radiates a post-coital glow from all the sex she's had this morning with Nick Stiel. She hums, going "la lahh lah la" under her breath, taking paper napkins and plates and plastic utensils from the basket and placing them on my desk. I wonder why she's so eager to play house with me. We've been lovers for years and she's never acted this way before. Why isn't she picnicking with the P.I.?

Obviously Eve's advent has also affected Lily. There are worry lines around her eyes but she smiles more easily and naturally. Her hair isn't fashioned into quite so tight a bun and she wears less layers though she still has a sweater on in this heat. Lily's not wearing her glasses and she's put a bit of rouge on her cheeks. She appears to sleep more deeply but perhaps for not as long. There's a little darkness under her eyes that I find strangely stimulating.

"Has that private detective been getting anywhere?" she asks, as if she doesn't know Stiel at all.

"I believe he has some leads."

"Really? Well, that's good for us. I expect that after all this time he should have some information dug up. What sort of leads are they?"

"I'm not certain. Maybe he's found something on where's she's from and how she got here."

Lily perks up at that but doesn't seem very concerned. Either she knows I'm lying or she thinks Stiel is feeding me false information in order to stay in Potts County with her. In any case, it doesn't worry her much.

"How are you and Eve getting along?"

"Very well. I enjoy her company. I was...lonely for a time, and I'm not any longer. She's a great comfort."

"Shouldn't we be preparing to make other arrangements?"

She looks up from laying out the food. "Arrangements? I'm not sure I understand."

"Foster care."

"No," Lily says flat-out, offering no chance for argument. "You want to hand her over to a social worker? Absolutely not. The poor thing's already lost and who knows what else she's been through. She doesn't need to be swallowed up by the system as well." She scoops potato salad onto all three plates and neatly places a piece of corn on the cob on each as well. This is as motherly as she's capable of getting and she's enjoying every minute of it. She pours a glass of milk for Eve.

"Has there been any trouble?"

"What kind of trouble do you mean?"

"Anything. Any problems?"

"No. None at all."

"Has she spoken yet?" I ask.

Eve continues to utterly ignore us. Lily has to think about it for a while, aggressively pensive as she clatters cups of macaroni salad around my desk. I'm prompted to reach over and shake her arm but I don't.

When she looks up at me at last Lily says, "She mutters sometimes. In her sleep."

"What does she say?"

"Who can tell? It's all just mumbling. Would you like some wine?"

"Sure."

From the basket she pulls two plastic glasses and a bottle of Chianti that's been sitting in a container of ice. She pours the wine and we sit sipping it, staring at one another. I think about the flat rock and what might happen if I brought Eve back to where she was found in the swamp. Maybe I should ask her about the dead kid and Herbie Ordell Jonstone's leg.

Undoing a button on her sweater, Lily presses the cool glass of wine to her cleavage. Her burgeoning overt sexuality is something of a turn off to me. "Sheriff Burke is completely inept. He hasn't been able to find out anything about her parents. All those computers and inter-office cooperation and still he's unable to learn anything. He even had the audacity to take her fingerprints."

"And there's no record of her anywhere?"

"No, of course not. Did you expect there might be? Do you think she's been in jail?"

"Sometimes parents print their kids just in case they're ever abducted. Has Doctor Jenkins taken another look at her?"

"No. Why?"

"It might be prudent."

"I think that's unnecessary, Thomas."

"All right."

"Is it costing very much? Paying for Mr. Stiel's services?"

"Don't worry about that."

"Well, come on, let's eat."

Eve doesn't turn from the window. I decide to try to shake something free. I get out of my chair and step up behind her, putting my hands on her shoulders. I'd hoped for some kind of reaction from the physical contact but there isn't anything. Perhaps she's used to men touching her. She completely disregards me, staring down at the factory floor like she owns the mill. I consider licking her all day sucker but I'm fairly certain that if I did we'd suddenly be locked in a death match, and I'm not quite ready for that.

She raps on the glass in exactly the same way the dead kid tapped on the door.

Lily takes out a glazed ham and puts it on the table.

IT costs a little over two hundred dollars to bail Dodi out of jail. Sheriff Burke takes the cash and hands me papers to sign but he doesn't let her free from the cell yet. He's got one boot up on the desk and is tilting backwards in his chair, relishing the moment. His hat is planted tightly on his nugget of a head.

Even though Sarah isn't pressing charges he considers this to be a big case that's broken wide open, and he doesn't want the attention to die down just yet. He's trying to come up with something that will be hip, street-smart and witty, with the proper amount of nonchalant jaded attitude, but so far he's dry. I can see him getting a little worried that he won't even be able to make the pretense. He wants to be a donut-eating hardass running in homicidal scum every day. He's watched enough cop shows and read a few true crime books—*Helter Skelter, Zodiac, Son of Sam*, all the stuff about Gacy and Dahmer, but nothing quite applies now and it's bugging him.

Burke takes some chaw out of his top desk drawer and bites off too large a piece. The miscalculation costs him as his mouth floods with too much juice. It drips down his chin onto his neat uniform and he winds up having to spit the whole thing out into his metal wastebasket.

Burke finally realizes he isn't going to utter anything funky and just says, "The Coots tramp coulda killed that girl. The hell's going on in your house? This never should have happened."

"It was sort of a territorial thing."

He leans forward trying to be imposing. "That supposed to be funny?"

"No."

"Took seven stitches for Doc Jenkins to close her up. That isn't funny."

"No, it's not."

"Another inch further in and she would've been spilling her guts out all over your fancy rugs."

Burke's never been inside the house and doesn't know if we have fancy rugs or not, but it sounds pretty good in the heat of his rant. Dodi wasn't trying to disembowel Sarah—the slash across her stomach had another meaning. Sarah is New York high class slumming as dog patch Daisy Mae, knotting her blouse at midriff, wearing the torn cut-offs. Dodi is the real thing and resents anyone intruding on her action. I find that understandable. She couldn't abide anybody mimicking what is hers by default. She was going for the pierced belly button, a sign of pop cultural iconoclasm that doesn't belong in the bayou.

But Burke is right about one thing. It never should have happened.

On the wall behind him are photos and statistics of all the dogs who've been kicked, including his own terrier, Binky. There's a close-up of Binky's tushy with the size twelve boot print on it. Binky and Burke look as if they may never recover.

"Those two gals can't stay in the same house any longer."

"You're right," I say.

"So what are you going to do?"

"One of them will be leaving."

"Which?"

"I don't know yet."

He's getting a little too excited and forgets to talk from his diaphragm. That fife-like piccolo voice eases from him as if he's been sucking helium out of a balloon. "There isn't much you do know, now is there?"

"Hm."

"That the only answer you got?"

His tone is getting to me. A light breeze circles his office and flaps the bills I've put on his desk. The chair creaks as he tips back again, stretching as if bored, about to yawn. He wags his boot towards me. There's an open window directly behind him. One shove against his desk and he'd flip right out of it.

"Have you found anything on Eve yet?"

"Who the hell is Eve?"

"The lost girl who's staying with Lily."

"Who said her name was Eve?"

"We had to call her something besides 'Hey You.'"

"She's none of your concern."

"Yes, she is."

"And who do you think you are hiring some shoofly from up North to come all the way down here to snoop into the middle of my investigation? You got so much money you feel like wasting it wherever you can?"

"Learn anything at all about the girl?"

"No," he says, trying hard to drop an octave and failing. "Let's stick to the subject at hand."

"How about the dog-kicker?"

"You never mind about him."

"He's tearing the town apart, that dog-kicker. People don't feel safe putting their own pets in the yard."

"Hey—"

"Can't leave them outside, you never know when the little dears are gonna get trampled upon."

"Shut up. I don't want to hear that crap."

"The kids, I think that's the worst part. It just isn't right that they should suffer so."

"That's enough."

"What it's doing to the poor children of Kingdom Come, seeing their beloved pets...."

It doesn't take much to put Burke on the defensive. He hops out of his chair like a boy rushing to watch cartoons and heads off to free Dodi. His boot heels tick against the tile floor making the same sounds as a scuttling rat.

Binky's photo stares back at me from the wall, full

of sorrow and anguish, with no promise of better days ahead.

I SEE that Fred's arm really has healed up nicely as he reaches out to shake my hand. He's gained a good deal of weight and all the manic tension has washed out of him, leaving him slow and sedate. He's apologetic about having stolen from me, but not overly so. He doesn't hold any hostility towards me and doesn't offer to pay me back. He probably doesn't remember much about that last night in the house anyway. Now he's got a sense of pride about him that he didn't have before. The rehab guys have done a fine job of whipping him back into shape.

He looks around for Dodi. He might be clean but he's still got the hots for her, that's natural enough. She's in another room, on the third floor, waiting patiently for Sarah to leave before showing herself again, as per my instructions.

It doesn't take long for Fred to get around to making his big movie pitch to me. Not the porn freaks flick he had all worked out but his new documentary on addiction. He foresees it as an eighteen part opus he wants to market to PBS. He unfolds a piece of paper covered with figures—costs, estimates and percentages—most of which I find rather reasonable. I tell him I'll carefully consider his proposal.

Sarah's on the phone with her father, whispering, the cord wrapped so tightly around her hands that it's a garrote. The sweet scent of honeysuckle sweeps through the house. A couple of long-jawed orb weaver spiders creep across the floorboards leaving fine threads of web behind. She says, "Yes, Daddy, I understand. Thank you, Daddy, I love you."

Staring at the photo of my parents that he'd tried to steal, Fred rubs his arm. He mouths words and I can read his lips. He's reciting the line I gave him before breaking his ulna, about how it would provide spiritual reassurance, a new hope for all. How he should take heart in that.

Maybe he does. But he remains an addict, and he starts looking around, wondering if I still have the better crystal I was cutting his coke with. His lips are still too wet and his tongue peers through them like a slug.

Sarah's bags are packed and she stands in the hall crying softly, looking back up the stairwell at the closed door of the bedroom. She's got her blouse tied at midriff, but the stitches on her belly are protected by a thick white bandage. It crinkles and snaps as she gives the house a last once-over. I think she'll miss it—us, Jonah, these preoccupations—for a while at least. Potts County can get in the blood. This distraction has been a rather intriguing one. It's presented her with lots of material to tell the shrink that her parents will have to hire. And the five grand in cash I've given her will help soothe some of her fleeting despair.

The tattooed masks of Tragedy and Comedy leer and grin at me as Sarah turns. She says, "Tell him—"

"What?"

"That it's best this way." Her voice breaks down the center. "It's time that I left. We...this...couldn't go on indefinitely. I'm sorry. I'm so sorry for all of it. Please tell him that."

"I don't have to. He's listening."

"Oh my God," she whimpers.

Fred is quietly opening and closing drawers, searching for the stash. Sarah brushes the tears off her chin and takes my hand. For the first time I feel a bit sad that she's going. The chemistry is changing once more, and we need to find a new equilibrium. She steps up on tip-toe as if to kiss my cheek but she doesn't. She glances into my eyes and smiles grimly.

"Take care of yourself, Thomas."

"And you, Sarah."

"Please watch over Jonah—all your brothers—as well."

"Of course."

"They don't need that girl, really. They need you."

She wheels aside and walks out. Fred babbles something about staying in touch, promising to send me some of his screeners, then grabs Sarah's luggage and follows her out the front door.

The screaming starts.

THAT immense brain is two-thirds wrath now, unbalanced as neurotransmitters slither and slosh and Cole's love diminishes in the misfiring synapses of heartbreak and rage. Sebastian is bitter and Jonah insane. Their hands are twitching, tongues unfurling, thoughts so distorted and loud that there's a buzz at the base of my neck and the hair stands on end. I want to see their eyes but every time I come close those gnarled arms and legs whirl and block me. I think about those powerful hands that gripped me in my nightmare, protecting me from the depths of the swamp and what waited to strangle me there. The lungs wheeze and hiss, growls bleeding through. Cole tries to speak reassurances but they won't let him talk.

There's no real poetry but the mouths mumble angry stanzas of indignation. They shamble and pirouette forward, the stunted distorted bodies quite beautiful and natural in their own way—the fluid angles and flesh of contorted bone, tendon and muscle are aesthetically elegant. The three shriveled forms merge to support the massive head, the unseen eyes, whirling and almost prancing. Sparks leap and pop across the carpeting. I speak Jonah's name and he withdraws to the corner, dragging the rest of the scuffling bodies with him, where they are all consumed by shadows. Fingers point at the door and I leave.

I'M parked outside of Doover's Five & Dime at around closing time when Lottie Mae's brother, Clay, and his buddy Darr pull in on their bikes. Cormorants, loons and grebes wallow and squawk in the green morass channels behind the store, waddling beneath the rotting docks where the swamp folk tie their poled skiffs when they come in to buy provisions.

Darr still has the butterfly Band-Aid on his forehead. The adhesive has worn off one edge and it flaps freely as he approaches. He hasn't bathed and the cut is crusted with dirt. He's a man who likes the world to take care of itself.

I wonder what the play is going to be. Clay stands and watches, arms hanging loosely at his sides, expressionless but alert. He glances at the door searching for his sister, unsure if she's still inside, or if, possibly, I've *done* something with her already.

Like Einstein, Darr doesn't waste time and valuable mental energy choosing different clothes each day. He's still got on the tight red sleeveless T-shirt, the jeans, boots, the belt buckle. One difference. He's tossed the tiny knife, probably in a fit of anger thinking the blade was a traitor after being cut by it, a defector to the enemy camp. It's the kind of thinking that leads men to call their guitars by women's names and eventually divorce them. He's got a new love, an eight-inch switchblade stuffed inside his left boot.

I get out of the truck and wait for him to step up. His belly keeps him pretty far off from me, but he's got the reach to make the distance. He cocks his head and the Band-Aid flops the other way as he stares over at the loons plodding along through the grass.

"You know what I simply cannot stand?" he asks me.

"I'll play along since this has the structure of a rhetorical question. What is it that you cannot stand?"

"Fencing."

I clear my throat. "Fencing?"

"Watching fencers who have no notion of the hardcore reality behind the art form. They think it's a sport, the damn fools. Or worse, some kind of performance they're putting on for their mamas, like ballet or synchronized swimming. It was never meant to be a sport. You've got to have convictions to live with the blade. Belief. True belief, that's it, that's what I'm talking about. But those *players*, they might as well be shooting hoops or sliding into third base. They never embrace the...the *tenets*, the *ideology* behind that discipline."

"I can't say that I have an opinion one way or the other."

"Trust what I'm tellin' you. No matter how much training they go in for they always got that swashbuckling bullshit fantasy going on in their heads. No way around that for most of 'em. They feel *gallant* sashaying around with their Musketeer sword, lunging after each other on the mats, shouting in French like it means somethin' special when they can't even pronounce the words. With those silly helmets on over their faces, you shouldn't be caught dead in one'a them, and the machines buzzing when they tap each other on the chests."

"Even the women?"

"Especially the women! Oh hell, don't get me goin' on that!"

He spits into the mud as the last couple of patrons leave the store and get back into their skiffs, stobpoling into the bayou. Lottie Mae turns the sign in the window to Closed and notices the scene out front. Vines drape against the glass and frame her face for a moment. She raises her chin and sets her lips into a thin white bloodless line before she withdraws.

Darr sways a little, maybe a sign of inner ear damage. "Wouldn't you think they'd get tired of that foolhardy act? All that idiotic fake valor they're supposed to be clutching hold of when they go prancing around like any old so and so? How you supposed to prove you're made of real blood and bone when you go stabbing at each other covered with all that metal get-up gear on, huh? Don't you think you'd get a lot further along if they didn't have caulk tips on the swords?"

"They'd probably try a lot harder not to get struck."

He bursts into a robust laughter which sounds genuine and a bit crazed. "That's it! You got it! My point, that's exactly my point right there!" His muscles ripple and the washed-out jailhouse tattoos look worse than melanoma.

I blink at him a couple of times and lean against

the side of the truck. Not only does Darr expect the world to handle itself but he's also got high hopes for the logic of his assertions to eventually come to validity all on their own. Maybe he's talking in metaphor. I wonder if this is some vague attempt at intimidation.

"I do believe you and me understand each other well."

"I'll get back to you on that," I tell him and walk over to Clay.

Maybe he's a conjure boy and he's already working spells and making invocations for purpose unknown, even to himself. His shoulders are drooped with weariness and his eyes are half-hooded. It appears that he has been through this—or something very much like this—many times before. I feel the same way.

"Why do you keep showing up around my sister?" he asks.

"The first couple of times she showed up around me, but I admit I came seeking her out tonight."

"Why?"

"I'm not so sure."

A small line appears between his eyebrows and it takes me a second to realize that this is his version of a frown. Then the line disappears. "Don't you have anything better to say than that?"

I think about it. "No, not really."

"You should probably stay away from her. I think that would be best." No implied caveat, no brandishing of weapon or muscle. His voice is slightly cold, traced with melancholy. I can tell that he once almost made it out of Potts County, only to be drawn back in.

"Did you come back to town for your sister?" I

ask. "To protect her? To take her out of here?"

"No."

"Why then?"

"Maybe I'll explain it to you sometime."

It's good to hear him telling the truth, flatly, without riddles. We'll get to the meat of the matter perhaps, if things turn out in a proper fashion, whatever the hell that is. We must wait for certain circumstances to play out, a chain of events that began with Lottie Mae's vomit, or maybe my grandmother on the school roof, or long before that even. Each incident following the other in a pattern that can't be determined yet. At least not by me.

I ask, "Does your friend really dislike fencing that much or was the whole thing some kind of roundabout threat?"

"No, he hates it."

"So why'd he tell me?"

"He likes you."

"Oh."

Darr takes out his switchblade, opens it and hurls it into the weeds at a passing cormorant. The bird shrieks in pain, rolls and flops and tries to crawl away as Darr goes after it.

There's very little blood. He stomps through the muck smiling, catches the duck and stabs it through the brain. He carries the corpse over and hands it to Clay, who handles the murdered bird with a certain reverence. Lottie Mae comes out with a croker sack, refusing to meet my eyes. I watch with mild fascination. Clay puts the dead cormorant in the sack, ties it shut and places it behind the seat of his bike. He and Lottie Mae get on his motorcycle, Darr gets on the other Harley, and they all ride away without another word.

I stand around for a while longer, thinking about Drabs and looking into the glowing green of the bog. The grebes and mallards float past, dipping for fish. A cold wind starts blowing and it feels good against my throat. Bull gators roar out in the morass and a few cormorant feathers drift by.

The loons weep, just as my mother wept, echoing through the lowland. I light a cigarette. Rising swamp gas ignites and flames spring and dance across the stagnant water, flailing and sinuous, writhing and red like dying men unwilling to let go of a hated life.

CHAPTER EIGHT

THE Crone and two of the other granny witches somehow get into the house one late afternoon and start running around performing rituals all over the place. They rush from room to room spattering foul-smelling oils across the doorways, chanting and carrying out cleansing ceremonies.

Strangely enough they pass by the bedroom where Dodi lies with my brothers trying to draw Jonah back from the abyss of his depression. They don't aim their prayers there and don't waste their potions.

Velma Coots hasn't sanctioned this attack. It's not her way. She, out of all of them, knows better. This faction of conjure women has broken off from the rest of the whole, rising out of the swamp after much planning on their part. When I come near they shriek words I don't understand and make warding gestures in front of my face. They believe there is a dark truth hidden here that must be excised immediately, and they've finally decided to take matters into their own hands. I can appreciate that kind of bravado. They wear their shawls, lace wrapped three times around their hair, bracelets of thistle and flower petals, carrying charms and bells that they ring every so often between all the yelling.

The Crone tires quickly and reaches out for the velvet draperies, sits on the divan, breathing heavily. She's too ancient to have a name any longer. When she coughs you can hear the ages rattling inside her shrunken frame. No human names can cling to her anymore—they slip from her dusty shriveled flesh like a young girl's whimsies. She holds star charts that show an alignment—a misalignment—of the planets and moons. Bloody streaks have dried across the parchment as if she's tried to compel the celestial bodies back on course through the force of her own soaking blood. I suppose it's as good a try as any.

I decide to make tea and offer them finger foods and pound cake. The Crone's voice is so brittle that it sounds as if it has been broken and repaired with a hammer and nails many times before. "You're culpable," she says.

"So you old ladies keep telling me. The more I hear it the less I believe it though, to tell you the truth."

"Dues a'plenty but it ain't your fault, not entirely."

"Yeah?"

"Sometimes it's just the way things are. Wrong, but natural."

"Well, thanks for that much. Pound cake?"

"Okay."

Her rags are paper-thin, held together only by filth, but she's swathed in them as if wrapped in gossamer. There's something very beautiful about all her stacked up years, vicious and startling as well. She deserves reverence and respect and I do my best to keep from throwing them out on the lawn.

"What's this shit you're tossing all over the place?"

"Oxtail soup, boiled for three days."

"Christ!"

"We thought it might help."

She says it sadly because she realizes it won't. We're beyond such measures and probably always have been. Her hands tremble as she takes the proffered tea cup and a slice of cake.

"I appreciate the effort. A little lemon?"

"Yah, please."

I add a slice of lemon to her tea and watch her eat with trembling hands. She gums the food until it's a thin gruel that swirls around her mouth for a time before she swallows.

My great-grandfather must've danced with her long ago. Thinking of it makes me a little rueful, about how it had been and how it should be. He danced with all the girls and plucked jasmine bouquets for each one of them when he did his courting, down Main Street and over the meadows, through the orchards and while walking to church. He had a good line, I guess. I look at her twisted brown fingers and imagine them pale and young again, drawn into his hands as they do-si-doed in the spring across the town square. That corrupted withered voice once tittered shyly as she whispered to him. The generations continue to close in.

"I'm old," the Crone says as if this should be news. "I don't have much consternation left in me. What I do got I reserve for the proper time, the right people and things."

"Me?"

She cackles and pieces of her clothing flake off. Her hair has come loose from her skull and nearly transparent strands waft to the floor. She's thin and tattered as a streamer caught in the wind. There's a madness circling in her eyes but it's a kind of insanity you can embrace. A madness of history and survival, much different than that of Drabs or Maggie or my brothers or even myself. Her voice fades in and out, weakening then gaining strength. She smells like bad meat.

"Most folks got secrets, but that ain't so with you."

"No?"

"Nah. It just ain't so. With you, well, it's the other way around. Them secrets, they come out of the wood, and they got you instead."

"Feels like it at times."

The other grannies drift outside and keep screaming and dancing and doing their thing. They pass in front of the windows fingering symbols onto the glass. I wonder if they tried contacting Lottie Mae and if she told them about the other night when she got drunk and wound up puking instead of making love to me, probing my underside for vulnerable spots.

"This pound cake is very good," she says.

"Yes," I tell her. "Dodi and I made it together."

"Didn't think that girl could cook a lick."

"She can't really. I did the baking and she mostly just handed me ingredients."

"Heard you liked to make bread." She frowns and glances up, for the first time aware of the soft noise filling the house from upstairs. It's like a hum on the edge of your ears that trills on and on. "What is that? Somebody weepin'?"

"Yes," I say.

She sips at her tea and even chews and swallows down the lemon slice. She turns again and gazes at the darkness at the top of the steps. "Who's crying?

That a ghost, you say?"

"My brother Jonah."

"He a ghost?"

"I don't think so."

She lets a belch rumble up and pats her stomach. "The boy's got some powerful blues."

"The love of his life just left him."

"When?"

"A week ago."

She rolls her eyes and her bottom lip droops. "If you gone sob like that for a solid week you'll never stop."

"I'm afraid you might be right."

She takes my hand and kisses it with her dry lips, gathers her belongings and folds the remainder of the cake inside her rags.

"The past can come back in a lot of different ways, chile. It don't get old and wind up buried like people do. It can die and be reborn. Sins take on shape and peck at your face."

"What do you mean?" I ask.

"You'll find out…"

"…soon enough. Yeah, I know. Tell me about the carnival."

The Crone frowns, displaying the gruel still stuck between her brown teeth, and says, "What carnival is that?"

MY father sits on the edge of my bed, staring straight ahead.

His evil is no longer molded with the face of his own life. He's free of that and with the dead-end destiny confining him to Potts County. He paid the price but he got out, at least in his own head. The arrogance is gone, his pride shattered. The living heart of his hatred has cooled to a weaker but more steady burn, and he doesn't seem to be familiar with anything around him. He could've left, I suppose, but he's chosen to stay behind. His vision and imagination have failed him long ago, but a desire to hold back the swamp has remained. He smells of stale sweat, moonshine, dog shit, spoiled chicken parts, and the bayou. Inadequacy and collapse. His ruin is complete, and from that he takes his freedom.

Leaves press harshly against the windows and the whippoorwills call. I want to ask my father if he's seen Maggie out there under the willows, but I'm afraid he might lie to me.

The phone is ringing downstairs and I have the overwhelming feeling that it's Drabs. He's being chased and can't hold out for much longer. I've got to pick up but I'm unable to leave the bedroom. My father's sitting on my legs as if he's trying to crush them. The phone stops in mid-ring and a deep-set moan rises from my chest. I want to kill someone but everybody's already dead.

My father murmurs my name, his own name. He still has his camera and he takes photos without aiming and without any flashes. I understand that this all has something to do with Maggie and not with my mother or God or Kingdom Come. Like any man, like any myth, he became jealous of that which would eventually replace him. He coveted what was mine. He loved her because he loved me and yet hated what I, like every son, represented. With the possible exception of my brothers.

Not his death or destruction, but his slow substitution and eventual erasure.

His evil has a new face now. Mine.

The camera clicks sullenly. He rises and steps to my brothers. His affection is evident in the way his eyes glitter with the tragedy of his tenderness. He is the hostage who, when finally released, cannot leave his prison.

He's no longer my size. He's grown much larger in his absence from us. I cannot fill his clothes and shoes. We don't take up an equal amount of displacement in this world anymore, and a vacuum has been created that must be filled. His void lives on, awaiting me in this room and under the bed, behind the drifting curtains, breathing heavily right next to me. I turn over.

Whoever she is, she's back again, doing fine and supple things to my lap. Perhaps this is the body of my sins. Her fiery red hair flares as shafts of moonlight spear down, piercing our dark corner. My father's shadow cuts across my chest, black and eternal, and I can't see her face although she's looking right at me.

Her faint noises aren't quite ecstasy or agony, but perhaps composed of both. My brothers moan in their sleep and she immediately quiets. She stifles her plaints against my side, where the face of my sister—what could have been my sister—had once been. She kisses the spot which is now scarred with Sebastian's teeth marks before taking me into her mouth again.

Someone—possibly me—wants to murder someone else, again possibly me. She drags her nails down my legs and then back up again, making other little motions as if she's scratching the words of oblivion into my skin. I try to decipher them. The silhouette of my father pinches its concealed chin, also attempting to read the wildly cursive script with all those well-defined curves. I keep catching the dotted "i," stunted "n" and hanging "g" of "ing" endings. She writes with plenty of active verbs. She's changed her narrative voice a bit since we first met in the back of my truck. Now there are more semi-colons and less of an emphasis is drawn to words via italics. Her paragraphs are shorter but there're just as many footnotes, and now she's added a comprehensive index and bibliography.

Suddenly I make out a few words. My father does too and grunts.

GRAVITY.

PENETRATION.

GRAVY.

MEANING.

SIGNIFICANCE.

I want to question her but I can't talk. My father waves his hands, vying for my attention but doesn't make a sound. I'm working towards an orgasm and don't know how in the hell that's happened. If she's touching me in some other deeper and delightful way then I can hardly feel it.

She's nearly finished with her documentation, these hexes. My father's shadow slumps but his sorrow isn't for me. I almost let loose with a gust of wild laughter. Whatever she's done here, perhaps it'll help us to progress to the next level.

I buck wildly into her mouth—what might be her mouth—and her tongue swirls and spins, tightening and loosening again. It's a damn nifty trick. I snort and hold tightly to her cold, stiff hair. She mutters and mumbles. I wonder if it's Eve here in my bed with me, veiled in the dark. My cum streams down her throat, if she has a throat. If it's Eve then I want to ask her to put on the bobby socks so we can start over and do this thing again. She talks through a mouthful of my vinegar calling somebody else, *something* else to come forth. She makes promises and demands, repeating nearly unpronounceable names.

The statements in my flesh have ignited again, and the room grows brighter. Her face remains wreathed in blackness. So does my father's. I expect some ancient and omnipotent presence to drag itself across the mire of time, up through the deep woods and morass of the bogs as it staggers towards the house.

I give it a few minutes, but nothing arrives and eventually the glow fades. She groans with worry, rises from the bed and opens the door. I reach for her but she turns away and gently shuts it behind her. I get the feeling that the next time she visits will be the last.

My father clicks his camera at me, then checks out the window to see if Maggie is there. I drop back against the pillows, waiting for the phone to ring again, hoping I'm only asleep and not as dead as my old man.

PRIVATE eye Nick Stiel is tearing up Leadbetter's. This sort of thing happens every once in a while and most of the men don't mind much. They've all gone through it themselves, more or less. This is custom. Ritual. But none of them are nearly as good at it as Stiel is. They stick to one end of the bar while Stiel performs a series of intricate martial arts moves and smashes tables, plunging his fists through chairs. This is pain in motion.

Deeder is a little miffed because he wants to shoot darts and Stiel has already torn the dart board in half.

Deeder has nothing left to aim at except the wild boar's head above, trying for the glass eyes, sometimes for the nostrils. Verbal Raynes has moved off beer and is now halfway through a bottle of Four Roses. He hasn't shaved in a week and nobody has been ironing his shirts for him. "God damn, I never thought I'd say this, but I miss Gloria! That Harry don't know how good he's got it."

The others respond with nods and pats to his back as they cram together in a small circle, doing their best to stay out of Deeder's range. He hasn't hit the boar head once but he keeps flinging darts all over the place. Verbal paws at his throat, counts through his change, and heads for the jukebox. He's played "Lucille" fourteen times in a row so far and no one has complained yet. It's that kind of night.

"She say she comin' back?"

"No, keeps telling me she don't ever want to see me again."

"You a hard luck man, Verbal."

"You speak the truth, friend."

"You miss her kids any?"

"Miss 'em? I still got 'em."

"You got 'em!"

"She and Harry done left all three of 'em with me. They goin' on a second honeymoon."

"I'm thinkin' that's some poor parenting on their part."

"I'm inclined to agree."

"No wonder she and Harry are lookin' so sprightly these last couple weeks. I thought it was just 'cause they were heading to the Caymans, but—"

"The hell's the Caymans? That near Gainesville?"

"Western Caribbean, a peaceful British Crown

Colony known as the Cayman Islands."

"What?"

"Consists of three islands just 480 miles south of Miami. The Grand Cayman, Cayman Brac, and Little Cayman."

"Goddamn!"

"Me and Deeder went down there once, few years back, after the insurance settlement came through for when we caught the Game Warden illegally tapping our phones."

"This over the Large Mouth Bass incident again?"

"Completely different set of circumstances, Verbal. About as clear cut a case of criminal search and seizure as you're likely to find. Them carp was in the tub for Rosh Hashanah, a traditional Jewish holiday, and for no other reason than that despite what they might say."

"You a Jew?"

"I was going through a phase."

The women eye Stiel and talk in hushed tones about him. Here's a real man who knows how to love and hate properly, but will take out his aggressions on inanimate objects, not you or your mother. His hands are bleeding and he enjoys the fact, smearing and licking his distended knuckles. It'll take a lot to rebuild the scar tissue but he's got to start somewhere.

He's smiling so hard that the corners of his mouth are cracked. Cigarette smoke twines about him and he turns and chops at it, thrusting, kicking. There's a beautiful sense of ballet to the violence. Lily's perfume is so heavy upon him that it bows his spine. The animal heads stare down and he glares back.

"How goes it?" I ask.

His neck is scratched. I recognize the little heal-

ing cuts—they've been made by briars. I knew he was
spending more time with Abbott Earl at the monastery but hadn't realized that he'd become a penitent as
well.

Stiel doesn't consider this display of brutality a loss
of control, and neither do I. He says, "I'm still on it.
You'll get your answers. I'm going to stay in town
until it's done."

"Maybe that's a bad idea."

He registers shock and freezes for a second, splin-
ters under his fingernails. "You want me off this
case?"

"No."

Relief loosens the hard edges of his face. He needs
that last vestige of self-respect and I've got no reason
to steal it away from him. Immediately his jaws tighten
again because he knows I'm about to ask about Eve.
He looks around for something else to beat up and
there's nothing left unbroken nearby. His eyes settle
on me and I wonder if we're about to get into it.

Stiel pauses and assesses me once more. "You're
not afraid of me, are you?" he asks.

"No."

"You scared of anything?"

"I don't know."

"If you were you'd know it."

"Maybe that's true."

Now it's time for the slow once-over, coming from
a guy with pink fingertips, his spirit torn apart by the
death of his wife and his seduction by a schoolteacher,
a detective who's stuck in a swamp town for no reason
he understands, tormented by a little girl driving him
out of his head.

"What the hell are you all about?" he asks me.

I think about telling him, *Shall I discuss my boyhood? Do you want to hear about the day when I let a child murderer die in the bayou?* But it sounds too orotund. I cross my arms and wait.

Deeder's dart comes sailing by. Stiel throws a fist at me that stops a quarter inch from my nose. It's a killing stroke. In the days before Lily scrubbed off his scar tissue he would've shattered my septum and driven it up through my brain. "Lucille" comes on again. We stare at each other.

IN my mother's dreams she is tugging at the coat sleeve of her father.

He ignores her as he's constantly done over the last three weeks since she returned with the news that Mama had been murdered. Except for the brief time he spent yelling at her for disturbing the bloody words on the school wall, he's said little.

He sits in a chair in the center of the living room, staring blindly ahead. Sometimes the radio is on, playing quiet music, but more often there's complete silence, like now. She yanks at his cuff and he doesn't respond. For a moment she fears that he's dead and she searches his chest for the handle of a reap hook.

There isn't any. The ends of his brown wiry mustache flutter lightly with his soft breath. Perhaps he is still angry with her for washing the evidence away, even if some of it was left behind. She does not mind blood and has had to kill a chicken and a pig over the last two days, but she can't stand the sight or smell of chalk anymore.

Perhaps this is all her fault. She apologizes once more and offers to make oxtail soup, his favorite. He doesn't answer. This is the worst he's ever been.

The drought continues and the dead fish stench works up from the bottoms and spreads throughout the entire house. She's grown accustomed to it by now and so have the parakeets, who peck at their water as the breeze brushes curtains aside and rattles the windows in their frames. Dust devils whirl past and the cottonwood trees dip and sway as if bending to peer down at her.

His face seems fleshless in the dying light, eyes sunken, lips parted so that his teeth appear as square and prominent as tombstones.

They have not been to her mother's grave. He would never go, she assumes rightly, and she feels that it's not safe enough yet for her to visit alone. The murderer and writer might not have left Kingdom Come, and could be lurking in wait for her almost anywhere. The swamp folk occasionally call to her through the kuzu and sparkleberries and try to warn her against certain places and people. They don't tell her anything she doesn't already know.

The sadness that has collected in her chest hasn't yet relented. Her mother had been laid open before the world and everyone now knows. This is almost as great a burden as dying itself. She is left behind without any reasons, without the substance of why this may have happened. She frets over the colored folks who've been lynched and had their homes burned down.

In the attic, a rat—or something—scampers. She's removed all the traps her mother kept stocked with molding cheese and poison. Mother had become almost obsessed with killing the creatures that did not belong here. It drove her into the attic at all hours of the night, carrying a broomstick, hunting and brushing out the corners. The rats—or whatever might be hiding—have their reasons and deserve to stay.

Father does not mind. Father doesn't mind anything anymore.

The granny ladies give her stews and thick teas to feed to her father, saying they will make him well again. She thanks the witches and takes the kettles home and pours their contents into the weeds. Sometimes the shrews will roll in the stuff and chitter madly to one another.

If her father is not dead then he is ill, and his sickness will end. He'll awaken and yawn, stretching and rubbing his belly, ready for another huge breakfast like in times past. They'll walk along the back roads of Potts County and eventually find themselves outside the gates of the cemetery. He will put his hand to her back and gently press her forward while he waits behind. She'll visit Mama's grave and say all the things she still has yet to say, and her mother will listen. Then Mama, perhaps, will tell her what must be told, and the simpering faces leering from behind the trees will recede into the night. Then everybody can get back to doing what they have to do.

She doesn't consider this another defeat. She forgives the shortcomings.

Father clutches at his heart as if sharpened steel has just gone through it. She moves along to sit on the porch and considers the man with three heads, who is waiting for her somewhere farther down the path.

THE phone is ringing again and I leap out of bed to nab it. Reverend Clem Bibbler wants to see me. By the time I get to the church it's two a.m. and Drabs' father is sitting in the back pew, praying in whispers.

I join him, listening to the rafters creak, the branches of white oak scraping against the shingles. You can imagine how it might have been forty years ago: the children opening their textbooks and taking out their pencils as my grandmother scratched equations and underlined conjunctions on the blackboard. Even with the reverend's prayers in my ear, staring at the cross and altar in front, with a missal at my side, I can get no true sense of this place as a church.

The room is no longer clean. There are wrappers, bottles, and remnants of half-eaten dinners strewn about. He's been staying here night and day in the hopes that his faith, his missing son or his absent congregation might return. Those two ropes leading up to the steeple snap and twist. The bell still rocks to and fro, and that constant thrum fills my chest and tries to get out through the top of my head.

The heat hammers at us but Reverend Bibbler still doesn't sweat. When he finishes praying he sits back and looks startled to see me here. He nods and the muscles in his black face shift unevenly beneath the skin. He looks as if he's trapped in the memory of something that's never happened. His stoic, impervious front has been penetrated. He licks his lips but his mouth is so dry that the tip of his tongue catches. "Oh, Thomas, please forgive me. I didn't realize you'd gotten here so quickly."

He doesn't find it odd that I would come out in the middle of the night at his request, and I don't find it strange that he'd ask.

"He was here," Reverend Bibbler says.

"Drabs came back?"

"Yes." He wrestles with whatever is crawling around in his brain, squeezing his eyes shut and repeating a litany as fast as he can. It's not helping and his breathing becomes brutally ragged. He might be having a heart attack. I crouch forward and put my hands on his shoulders and he snaps back as if he didn't know I was there. "Thomas, he was wounded."

A chill forms in the pit of my belly and keeps edging out, cooling me off inch by inch until I'm trembling. "How so?"

That all-prevailing silence washes over and engulfs us again. It always happens. I look down and see that I've picked up the worn missal. I page through it and I'm surprised that so many of the hymns are unknown to me. Belief and conviction are always changing and rushing along like the river. I should leave but he has more to say, and he's working his way up to saying it. I sit in the pew growing colder and give it some more time.

Something breaks loose inside him and a fierce and barbaric hiss works free. "They lynched him! Scalded him with tar again, but much worse this time. Rope burns around his throat, raw and infected—" He struggles for air, but can't breathe through his gritted teeth. "They...they...oh what they did to my boy. My son, my little boy...." He doesn't have to finish.

My teeth are about to break and I fling the missal as far from me as I can. "Oh my God."

"I don't understand how he survived."

But he does understand, and so do I. Drabs has always been watched over and used for another purpose.

"I failed him."

"We both have," I say.

"His voice has been destroyed, and the words that came out didn't sound human. But they were."

"Are you sure?"

He knows what I mean. "He didn't speak in tongues. He said the Holy Spirit had finally left him. He'd done all that he had to do. He was smiling, Thomas. Happier than I'd ever seen him. Laughing and making those horrible sounds. Scarred and bloody with his manhood mutilated, but he was joyful. Oh Lord in heaven forgive me, but it was wonderful to see him smile."

I had promised to find him and I had failed. I was more like my father than I ever wanted to admit. Failure inspired me just as much as anything else, and now it urged me to let out an enraged bellow that had nothing to do with rednecks or rope and everything to do with my own oversights and weakness. Reverend Bibbler puts a hand out to touch me and I shrink away.

There's a tap at the window.

I look over and see a smear of moonlight reflecting off the nutmeg skin, igniting the whites of eyes, blazing teeth.

Drabs peers in smiling, and Christ, it *is* a beautiful sight.

As he drops away into darkness I spin out of the pew and run after him.

Reverend Bibbler slides in his seat, sticks his foot out, and trips me. I go tumbling into the aisle and fall flat on my face. My chin cracks hard and suddenly blood is flooding my down my throat. I spit out a mouthful onto the wood floor.

I grab the reverend by the collar of his heavy frock coat and scream, "Why'd you do that?"

"Leave him be. He's happy now."

I rush outside and see a dark shape cavorting across the lawn, heading for the tree line. I scream his name and Drabs slows but doesn't stop. I sprint after him, watching the silver light lapping at his glistening wounds. He's letting me catch up. He's still naked and the kudzu must be tearing his feet apart, but he's beyond feeling pain now. His soul's been released. I stumble over a patch of crabgrass at the instant he breaks into the woods. I'll never find him in there and he knows it, so he stops for a moment, eyeing me.

"Drabs?"

He begins laughing feebly, and that destroyed cheerful voice is filled with a choir of ill children.

CHAPTER NINE

SISTER Lucretia Murteen's body is found in a ditch off the highway. Her uterus has been perforated and she's bled to death elsewhere, her corpse moved and hidden beneath the palmetto leaves. It looks like a botched abortion.

She carried invisible babies across an empty nursery but she'd never gotten the chance to bear her own. Abbot Earl is inconsolable at the funeral, as are several other monks and sisters who belong to the order. Many of the seekers and travelers also show up to pay their respects.

More people from town turn out than I expect. As a whole, the folks of Kingdom Come haven't embraced the new faith or those who follow it. But Lucretia Murteen is one of their own, or had been, and for the sake of the woman they'd once known they pay their respects.

Hundreds show up in the blazing sun. Some with lemonade, lawn chairs and sandwiches, and others have even brought along their pets. There are many children running among the tombstones, saying prayers, holding flowers. They read epitaphs and show off their kittens, giggling with delight. Sister Lucretia would've enjoyed that, I think.

We must wait for sixth hour before commencing. Abbott Earl has a long eulogy prepared, but he can't calm down long enough to give it. He grabs anybody near him and holds on for life—his powerful muscles strain as he hugs everyone tight enough to cut off the blood flow. His sobbing is as loud as a fire engine.

Abbot Earl is pulled away and leaned against a cottonwood tree, which he immediately begins to throttle. Another monk is forced to speak instead. He does a fair job under the circumstances even though he speeds through the service, dry-mouthed and occasionally quivering.

She is buried wearing the eye patch, not very far from my grandmother's grave. The pilgrims wander the grounds, searching out spirits, God, death, redemption or resurrection. It's a respectable cause. Several are performing their own strange rites, clanging tiny bells and waving incense, dancing in circles. Most of them continue to wear the cowls and robes of the penitent.

A couple conceal bottles of gin and tequila in their shapeless garments, taking furtive sips when they think no one is watching. A few others are just tripping on acid and talking about the groovy colors in the sky, pulling at their melting faces. Deputies chase after the naked ones who are running around in the woods. Some of the folks turn their lawn chairs around and watch the antics.

Those travelers must've seen a thing or two in the middle of the night at the monastery. Even while stumbling over roots and rocks they mime the same motions that Sister Lucretia Murteen once did. It's bad form but I need a cigarette and light up. The acidheads act as if they're walking down a long hallway handing newborns to mothers in the maternity ward. They sit talking with phantoms for a time, discussing the beautiful infants, those bright and open futures.

Daylight runs into their mouths as they turn blindly to face me, arms wide.

Burke is taking notes and doing little else. The sheriff's seen movies where they say the murderer might show up at a victim's funeral. He hasn't thought ahead enough to bring a camera so he can take photos. He's writing down names, license plate numbers, checking shoe sizes. Binky shall be avenged.

Abbott Earl cries himself dry. He hits the wall and once he gets there he simply can't weep anymore although he wants to. He wipes his face with his robes and the sewn-in catclaw briars crease his cheeks with scratches.

There are three people in town known to perform abortions—two farmers' wives and Velma Coots. Planned Parenthood is simply too far away, too expensive, and nobody in Potts County can trust a stranger in such matters. We stick closer to home.

I've brought girls to all three of them before and none would have screwed up the job as badly as I've heard Lucretia Murteen's abortion had been botched. Either somebody else has decided to try their hand at it or Sister Lucretia did it to herself. Still, someone had to dump and cover her body.

Abbot Earl is so drained by now that he can barely stand up under his own power. Two monks take hold of his arms and steady him as best they can. He sways and finally regains some of his composure. They try to lead him to shade but he won't go. He spots me far in the back alone, on the embankment, and makes his way over, hiking his vestments up so he can climb.

"I need to speak with you," he says. His voice is wet and heavy, sloppy and full of misery, but there's something tough down the center of it. If my father had ever had that hardness he wouldn't have killed himself.

"I'm listening."

"Yes, this is difficult for me...."

I'm forced to back away a step. I hadn't been close enough before to smell the vodka on his breath. Sister Lucretia's death has drop-kicked him back into the old pattern of drinking through his pain just like when he worked for my father trying to clear the swamp. The shallow cuts on his face well up and drip. We stand beneath the darkening sky looking at one another. He starts tapping his incisors together again, that nervous tic coming on strong.

I tell him that I suspect Sister Lucretia had been having an affair with one of the spiritual seekers staying at the monastery, a different man named Sebastian. He shakes his head until it nearly wags off his shoulders and says that there is no man named Sebastian staying at the Holy Order of Flying Walendas, and never has been.

"Are you positive?" I ask.

"Yes."

He still thinks that I'm somehow involved, of course. It's justifiable. A niggling worm of suspicion can eventually chew through your sleep. He heard her mention my brother's name while she was praying and he feels Sebastian has—in some unfathomable way— something to do with her death. Perhaps he does.

"Talk to me, Earl," I urge. "What happened to her?"

"There's not much more I can tell you or anyone else. Whatever happened to her occurred during the night. I said goodnight to her myself and watched her go to her chambers. The next morning she didn't come to meet us for breakfast and morning prayers."

"Do you still believe she wanted to leave the order?"

He lets out a sigh that fogs my face with vodka. "She had grown more and more distant."

"That doesn't necessarily mean anything."

"I know that."

Unconsciously, he inches his hand out as if to grasp my wrist. He's in dire need of human contact but he's afraid to get too close to me. He wants my help but he's hoping to avoid asking for it directly. "The last time we spoke you mentioned she might have been going because she felt threatened."

"Yes, I said that."

"Do you still think that's the case?"

"I believed someone might have been imploring her to leave us. Possibly her lover, whoever he might be."

"It makes sense."

"Yes, perhaps he wanted to marry her and raise a family. Or...maybe he was simply afraid of being found out and—"

"And forced her to get an abortion."

He can't help himself any longer and finally grips hold of my arm. I have to suck my breath between my teeth. He hangs his head and when he glances back up the veins in his neck are standing out, thick and red. "My God, I can still hardly believe it. For her to be left like that."

"Does Burke have any suspects?"

Abbott Earl suddenly seems embarrassed. "I'm afraid that in my grief—"

"You mentioned me and my brothers. It's all right."

He lets go of me and the iron is back in his voice. "Sebastian. She spoke the name Sebastian. I heard her clearly." He uses his robes to wipe the blood and sweat from his face but he only tears it up some more. A cut at the corner of his mouth opens wider and the salt in his sweat must sting him horribly. "I'm sorry. Perhaps I never should have said anything at all."

"Don't worry. Burke hates me enough to put me at the top of any of his lists of suspects."

"He doesn't hate you, Thomas, he admires you. And we're often frightened and jealous of what we admire."

I think he's giving me and Burke a little more credit than we deserve, but I let it go. "Could they tell how far along she was?"

"The doctor said ten weeks. They only know for certain because the fetus was still intact. Can you believe such a horrific thing? *That's* how incompetent this...this person was."

The funeral is over and folks are beginning to leave. They drop their flowers and say a few last words over Lucretia Murteen's coffin, fold up their aluminum lawn furniture and head home again. The pets need to be fed. The tiny ringing bells stop and the incense fades away on the breeze.

Watching, Abbott Earl grimaces. The grave appears very small and lonely now and it pains him to see it that way. "I don't have much confidence that the sheriff will ever find anyone to hold responsible for this tragedy."

"I doubt it too."

"I'm going to ask that private detective to look into these matters. I hope you don't mind."

It strikes me then that Nick Stiel hasn't been in attendance. Neither has Lily or the girl Eve. "I understand that you've become friendly with him."

"He's a good man with a great burden of sorrow. I only hope he's able to come to grips with it."

"I do too."

I'm about to ask him how much he knows about Stiel's relationship with Lily and the girl from the flat rock when he says, "I heard about what happened with Drabs Bibbler. I'm very sorry."

It stops me. "How did you...?"

His gaze is downcast and he does something that I haven't seen anybody else do in years: he blushes. I realize then that one or more of the men in the lynching party must have gone to Abbott Earl for some sort of absolution.

In a heartbeat the consuming rage is on me like a wild animal tearing at my back. My field of vision fills with white spots and a pleasant lightheadedness comes over me. I want to hang onto it for a minute but almost immediately it's gone. I lunge as if to shake the names out of him but I stop myself before I grab his throat.

A breeze wafts his awful breath at me again. I choke on it and force my fists deep into my coat pockets to prevent me from choking the identities of those bastards out of him. My tie flaps over my shoulder like a whip beating at me. A snarl stays low in my throat. I never let it out but it's there all the same.

He knows the murder in me and it doesn't alarm

him. He's seen it many times before—in himself, in my father, maybe in every man. His tongue juts and I want to tear it out by the root.

He says, "No, Thomas, nobody confessed to me, if that's what you're thinking. I met with the reverend in his church. He needs solace as well. That poor man. That poor sad boy of his."

I'm not sure if I buy it. It's the end of sixth hour and a calmness descends upon Abbott Earl along with his silence. He turns and walks away, followed by the rest of the order.

I stand alone. My hands remain still in my pockets, and I still want to strangle somebody.

ONE of the naked acidheads in the back seat of the cruiser is on a trip that's begun to go bad. He shrieks and fights against the shackles, smashing his nose open on the window. Burke starts to approach me but stops, looking back and making little jittery motions like he has to go pee. He isn't sure if the deputies can handle somebody like that, and he keeps yelling at them to bring the crazy bastard to Doc Jenkins, who also won't know what to do with him.

Sheriff Burke holds his hand up in a "stop" gesture at me even though I'm not going anywhere. The deputies start to drive off but they've got to hit the brakes and stop short when sixty-eight-year-old Maybelle Shiner rushes in front of the car and begins doing an impromptu striptease on the cemetery lawn.

Somebody's spiked her lemonade. She's sprightly for a geriatric and sprints for the front gate, tossing off her black shawl and pediatric pumps as she zips along. She charges past me in a blur and Burke screams, "Stop her!"

She flashes her flaccid breasts at me as she flies by and says, "Freedom! Happy day!"

"Nice tits, Maybelle," I tell her.

What the hell.

Burke gives me a glare of unbridled loathing and goes after her as the deputies trundle up the meadow hill. Maybelle's got them by at least twenty yards now and is stretching her lead. It's fascinating to watch. Burke can hardly run at all in those oversized boots and he's got one hand on top of his head trying to hold his hat on. I look around to see if anybody else is catching this but everybody's gone.

The crazed naked guy in the cruiser smears his bloody nose against the glass and keeps nodding me over. I walk to the patrol car and stand there staring at him.

He's pretty furry. Overgrown beard and a wild mustache with thick thatches of hair on his chest and shoulders. I'm grateful I can't see his back. His nose gushes. He's maybe thirty but already there are spots of gray showing through and he's got cigarette burns all over. A sure sign that he falls asleep smoking and will go out of this world in a fireball. His eyes blaze with a raw eagerness to get something accomplished. Straining at the cuffs, his bony clavicles stand out harshly beneath the fuzz. If he keeps going like this his shoulder blades will crack.

"I think you better calm down a little," I say. "You're only going to hurt yourself."

"I know you! I know you! Brother Thomas! You're—"

His face is a crimson splash with flaring nostrils. He bashes the window some more and I can see that his nose will have a permanent tilt down and to the left from now on. The two other naked guys back there are in the happy zone, mellow and sort of swooning. They're having a quiet but intense discussion about butterflies and cyanotic children suffocating because of their umbilical cords.

Maybelle has made a buttonhook move that would put Johnny Unitas to shame, completely outmaneuvering Burke and both deputies, zigging and zagging among the tombstones.

I feel like clapping but I don't want to take my fists out of my pockets just yet. I'm not sure what'll happen and don't feel like finding out. She's tossed all her clothes by now and I wonder what the hell is in the LSD that makes everybody around here suddenly want to strip and streak.

Fuzzy is getting even more excited and now he's torn a gash above one eyebrow that has him blinking madly. "Brother Thomas!"

"Listen, you need to relax and ride it out. Don't fight. In a few hours you'll be okay."

"You are Brother Thomas, the breadmaker, aren't you?"

He's a fan of my baking. Twenty minutes of kneading the dough does the job. Plus the raisins, they all like the raisins. "Yes."

He has to spit blood out before he can say anything more. "The lights, all these lights—"

I admit, it perks me up. I lean in closer. "Carnival lights?"

He frowns and looks at me like I'm nuts. "The hell you talking about, man, you stoned? These are God's lights!"

"Oh."

"God's here and he's got a message for us all."

"Of course he does."

He catches sight of Maybelle rounding a sumac. "Damn, look at that old lady's tits flopping around! I hope they catch her soon, that sort of thing offends me. I mean, it's just rude to crank up an old lady like that! One of these assholes here must've turned her lemonade on."

He's still struggling wildly against the high tinsel steel bracelets but there's absolutely no exertion in his voice. The tiny bones in his wrists, elbows and shoulders are cracking and popping loose. He's going to need an entire upper body cast when they finally get him to a hospital.

"Goddamn, Brother Thomas, there's a Ferris wheel. It is a carnival! The carousel is whipsawing around and all the horses are black, their eyes crazy, ruby-red, vicious. They've got horns too, not unicorn horns but more like goats. Like the devil's! How did you know?" He snaps his head around and more blood splashes against the glass. "Hey man, before I forget to mention it, I love your bread. The raisins, man. Most monks can't bake for shit but you've got the touch."

"Thank you."

He shuts his eyes, looking at something deeper inside himself and not liking it. His temples tighten and throb, even his eyelids are quivering as he grits his teeth and flops back in the seat. "Ah, hell. Some skanky dude here wants a drink."

"What?"

"Oh fuck! What's he doin' with that snake? Jesus, that's twisted! I'm gonna be sick."

There's a loud snap and for an instant I think he's actually managed to twist the cuffs off. But that isn't it at all. His left arm has given out and a jagged stake of bone is poking through. He glances at it, gives a manic titter, falls back against the seat and passes out.

The other two guys continue their heated discussion, which has moved on to Victorian literature, namely the poet Dante Gabriel Rosetti and the pages of verse he buried with his wife, only to dig her up again years later. Fuzzy slumps sideways and bleeds all over the dude. They don't seem to notice much.

Maybelle makes a bad turn and falls headlong into Lucretia Murteen's open grave. She lays on top of the coffin laughing wildly and, from the sounds of it, thumping her head. Burke doesn't want to go down there and get her and the deputies appear very uncomfortable about the entire afternoon's events.

I collect her clothes, walk down the hill, jump into the grave and ease Maybelle up until Burke can haul her out. Burke takes her home and the deputies drive off with the three naked guys in the back seat. Nobody's left in the cemetery except me and the gravedigger, who fills Sister Lucretia's grave the old-fashioned way, using only a shovel and the muscles in his back.

I look around for Maggie, scanning the distant cottonwoods. I don't see her but I know she's here someplace, along with many of my ghosts. I can feel her nearby and I want to ask her to protect me again, to guard me through these dark hours, but I can't even manage to call her name.

THAT night when I saw my father sitting on the edge of my bed, snapping photos from out of the depths of hell, was the last time I slept in my—my brothers'—bedroom. After that they shut the door to me and I've seen no reason to force my way in.

The tension can be felt throughout the whole house, and my side hurts constantly now. But the time is approaching when we'll have to face each other again. We are all very patient men. Dodi continues to care for them during the day, but she spends most nights with me. She's usually asleep when I come to bed and she's gone by the time I awaken.

Tonight, though, she's waiting for me.

Another storm is brewing. I can feel the heavy pulse inside my bones and far in back of my eyes. Thunder groans in the roiling silver-laced clouds, and lightning occasionally dips over and hits the swamp like a striking viper. The rain comes softly at first, and the sweet scent of mimosa and loblolly pine drifts on the wind. My mother's curtains rustle and sweep across my bare shoulder.

"It's back," Dodi says.

The restrained terror in her voice works against me in all the wrong ways. Her heavy breath is tinged with good scotch. She's never taken a drink in front of me yet but she can hold her liquor well. Now come the chants and the invocations and all that shit about my vinegar again. "You can't expect to go through the rest of your life and never see rain again, Dodi."

"This is different. It's gonna get bad, just like before."

"No, now listen to me—"

"The river's gonna flood, people will be drowning face down in the parking lots and gutters. Bog town gonna fall into the swamp. You jest watch. The dead get up, the past comes around again. Mama says—"

"I don't care what your mother says."

"Yes, you do, Thomas, though you don't want to confess it. I done told you once. This is a storm of souls. That's what she calls it, and I see no reason to argue with that a'tall. Neither should you."

"I'm not arguing. I'll handle things in my own way."

"How?"

"Shh."

"But how?"

Dodi is afraid of listening to all the gurgling, sluicing water pounding at the roof. That thumping at the walls is too much like the knocking of the dead and doomed just waiting to come inside. It seems like such a long time since she's run across the yard in her cotton summer dress and swung on the old tire hanging in the yard while the rain darkened her hair and splashed down her legs.

She smoothes herself against the mattress, sheets twining tightly around her body, her breasts damp and shining white in the dim light.

"The ghosts, they coming back."

I say something to her that I know I shouldn't, but it's like a whisper that's been forced out from inside. "They've never left."

"More fool you then to deny what's happenin'. It wants us. It's always wanted us. Everybody, the whole town."

There's no point in continuing this way, we're not getting anywhere fast. "You want me to go see your mother again?"

"I'm not sure. I thought maybe she'd know what to do, but now I ain't so certain. Mama's strong in her ways but...."

"But what?"

"Well, the truth is she can't fight this too good no

more. She's down to only six fingers."

"Jesus Christ!" I blurt out.

She nods, shrewdly, cannily, aware of more than she should be. She rubs her feet together like a little girl. "I'm just talking because I need to, that's the only reason. I don't mean to unsettle you none."

"It's all right."

The familiar sound of branches tearing at the shingles consoles me in some odd fashion. It reminds me of the nights when my parents would make a fire and we'd sit in the glow of the television screen taking comfort in each other's company. Rain splashes and murmurs. Dodi reclines against the pillows, drawing me forward onto the bed. I move beside her, and she groans and pulls me closer. When I try to press her legs open her small fist comes up to my chest like a rock and stops me. I wait, listening to the growling in the skies. I like the sound.

"You're the only one who can save us," she tells me.

"Shh."

"Stop shushing me, dammit."

She lays back, displaying her thick but well-trimmed pubis mound. She squirms a bit but not from desire. A harsh frowning line appears between her eyes. From her position she can look out the window and see the distant tracks of lightning at work in the bayou. Her hand slides over her belly, ranging across the silken loveliness of her pale, cool skin.

"Will you save us?"

I need affirmation too. It's why we're here. A whippoorwill calls and she flinches so forcefully that she cracks the back of her skull on the headboard. She rubs the spot and her hair is suddenly wild and unruly. I find that deliciously erotic and my breath grows heavier. She glances up at her own shadow on the wall, brushing her riotous curls out with her hands.

"Thomas—"

"I don't want to talk about it anymore tonight."

"It ain't your choice."

But it is. I press myself towards her and mash her lips with mine. She moans out of annoyance and not passion, wanting to scold me some more. In another part of the house my brothers are angry. Jonah's poetry is caustic and piercing but no worse than Sebastian's laughter. Cole's love is the love of the night-world and he alone understands the true liberty of darkness. The water on the window throbs and streams, reaching like splayed fingers.

I shut the light and Dodi halfheartedly protests once more, mewling louder and perhaps shedding tears against my chest. Maybe it's only sweat. The storm keeps rolling in. I take what I'm after. Thunder settles on the property. Poetry be damned. Let them grouse in their dirty corners.

THE dead kid is walking around the back yard again, and this time he's brought Herbie the child-murderer with him.

The rain drizzles in gentle waves, wind nudging it to part here and there. Our lawn is flooded and covered with large puddles six inches deep in places, like miniature ponds. Mallards and ducks will have a good time swimming in them tomorrow morning. The cypress and willows swing and crackle, like old men laughing. Johnny's mouth drips skimmer dragonflies and Herbie carefully avoids them, crutching his way across the grass. They're having a quiet conversation, laughing a lot, Johnny nodding heartily in agreement. When he does, the mosquitoes fly from his lips and a dark cloud wreathes his head. Herbie is good on the crutches, fast, and he manages to skitter away before he can get bitten.

It's a thing to watch. Herbie has his trouser leg pinned up to the stump and wrangles ahead easily. He looks twenty years older but just as powerful. Those arms have broken the back of a bull gator and I figure he's still strong enough to do the same now. It gets me smiling a little.

I put on my pants. I remember how embarrassed I was last time when I went downstairs naked to meet with Johnny Jonstone. I take the steps three at a time and turn the corner into the kitchen, waiting to see my brothers.

Instead, Sarah reaches up for me from where she sits on the floor beneath the phone.

"Don't go out there, Thomas," she tells me.

"Sarah," I whisper. I get the vague sense that this isn't how things are supposed to be, but I don't follow up on it. Still, I'm curious. I touch the back of my skull and wince and she does the same. "What are you doing back here?"

"They won't let me go," she says, her voice heavy with anguish. "Not just Jonah. All of them."

"But you left with Fred."

"No, not quite."

I cross my arms and lean against the cupboard. The stitches in her belly have gotten infected and the skin is raw and torn around the thick white bandage. There are wads of cash scattered around her. I'd guess it's the five thousand I paid her to leave. They've sent her to haunt me because my conscience has failed to do so.

"Where are they?" I ask. "Where are my brothers?"

"They won't help you anymore."

"I figured that."

She reaches up to the phone and pulls the receiver down with her, and I can hear a harsh buzzing, possibly a voice, emanating from it. A couple of long-jawed orb weaver spiders creep across the floorboards leaving threads of web against her legs. She says, "My father hates me. He wants to fuck me. It's worse now than when I was a child. He wants me dead."

"Sarah, don't listen to...to whatever you're being told."

"You don't understand!"

"It's all lies. Your father loves you. He always has. Everything's all right. You need to go home now."

She shakes her head. The tattooed masks of Tragedy and Comedy leer and grin at me, and their mouths are full of blood. "I never should have left. Fred's just going to get wired again, there's no way he can break his habit. He burgles houses and sells whatever crap he can. He's in and out of rehab every few weeks. I belong here. I love Jonah. You all need me."

"You might be right," I say, "but you still have to go. Your parents care about you. You've got a life waiting."

Her nostrils are red and cracked once more. Maybe she's back on cocaine or maybe that's merely how Jonah wants her to be—broken without him. He keeps her tangled up in our minds.

The murdered boy is at the back door gesturing me to come outside. The scent of sweetgum trails inside and the rain makes the world smell clean. There are more black fingerprint marks around his neck, as if Herbie has been practicing over the last couple of days, trying to get back into shape. Johnny raps at the screen door exactly the same way that Eve tapped on the glass in my office. He leaves behind a smudge of crushed milkweed bugs.

Sarah says, "Thomas, can't you feel it, can't you get a whiff of it? Stay out of the yard tonight."

"You people are always telling me that."

"Follow good advice," she cries. "They told you once that the man isn't dead. He's come looking for you. Go run and hide."

"I'd rather get to the bottom of this and be done with it."

"You'll never be done with it, don't you know that?" The buzzing on the phone is getting louder but I still can't hear any distinct words. "You'll just wind up deep in the swamp again."

"Maybe that's a good thing."

"Don't you believe it. You're—"

"—no longer safe, I know. Everybody's said it. But I still think it's time Herbie and I had a discourse."

"He doesn't want to just talk."

"I know that. Hang up the phone."

"No, I can't, I've been trying...." She grips the receiver so hard that the plastic case is cracking.

"Go back home, Sarah."

"But my father. He hates me! He wants to screw me. He has ever since I was a little girl. His eyes, you should see them, they're always bloodshot and on fire, like roadside flares burning. Oh God, if only you could see his eyes." She presses her mouth to the phone. "Hello? Yes, Daddy...."

"That's somebody else talking, Sarah. Who is it? Jonah? Sebastian?"

"Let me stay with you," she pleads.

"No."

I grab the receiver out of her hand and put it to my ear. The buzzing of voices has stopped but I can still hear breathing on the line. I hang it up and walk to the back door. Johnny's gone, and when I turn back I see that the phantom Sarah is too. Spider web strands flutter to the kitchen floor.

I walk out the back door into the yard.

The night is slick as crude oil. The rain continues to fall and it feels good against my heated forehead. It's as if I have a fever, but I'm not ill. The pain in the back of my skull begins to recede. I brush my curls out of my face and I hear my mother calling after me, high-pitched but not quite wailing. Mama has enough of her own troubles. I don't bother to look for Maggie or Drabs hiding in the brush. They're not there. For the first time in my life I feel completely alone, and I'm not sure what to make of it. Mist swirls at my ankles as I wander across the muddy grass. Herbie's here someplace, come back to put the squeeze on me.

CHAPTER TEN

THE moon's a wet smear across the crashing, boiling clouds. Silver bleeds down against the wind-swept, shuddering trees. Cottonmouth snakes slither beneath the cabbage palm and shagbark hickory, tails slapping hard in the water.

If he hadn't been smiling I wouldn't have seen him.

But Herbie Jonstone has waited nearly twenty years for this and the glee makes him show off his nice white teeth. The moonlight catches in them like peanut brittle and I turn a second too late.

He's good with the crutches, all right. Two decades on one leg will do that for you. Before I can completely wheel around and face him he's driving one crutch hard into my solar plexus. I squeal and go down to my knees in the marsh grass.

"Been waiting for a long time to see you again, boy."

His teeth are clean but his breath is bad. Smells like he's been eating undercooked possum in the deep woods for a while now. No shower for a week and the rain isn't helping much. If he'd been downwind of me I would've gagged on his B.O. five minutes ago.

When I finally get enough of my breath back to speak I say, "Been...in the same house all...my life. You could've come visit from Tupelo...any time you wanted to, Herbie."

His tremendous arms bulge again as he tightens his fists around the rubber grips. His palms creak harshly against them as loud as the twining ropes of the church bells. "I been meanin' to, but I sorta got sidetracked. Life throws us curves, it does indeed. Got caught doin' somethin' sorta unfriendly to somebody and had to do some time in Angola."

He's not afraid of me running off. He knows we're here for a reason and neither of us is about to shirk that obligation now. I find that I'm actually interested. "How long were you on the Farm?"

"Fifteen years. It wasn't bad though, 'cept I missed the kids."

"I bet you did."

I dive for his leg and he brutally swats me aside with a crutch. It catches me hard across the mouth and my throat runs with blood. He reaches down, grabs me by the neck, and hoists me into the air. Christ is he quick. His huge arms are solid as wrought iron, and despite his unfriendly intentions, I'm impressed. I grasp at his fingers trying to loosen their hold but can't even move them an inch. He draws me in close until we're almost nose to nose.

He could collapse my trachea in an instant but he doesn't. He's a talker and wants to make it last for a time. "You got anything you want to get off your chest in the sight of God, son, 'fore you die?"

As a matter of fact, I do. "A few things."

He chuckles warmly and I find myself almost liking him. It's no wonder he can cull the kids so easily.

"Well, let's hear some."

"Why didn't you kill me that day? You didn't bleed out and the gators didn't roll you down under the river."

"No, they surely did not." He cocks his head, slack-jawed, staring deeply into me until the rain dribbles over his lips. He's got to spit out a mouthful of water. "I barely had the strength to pull myself to the opposite shore. Oh that was low, son, leaving your belt on the other young'n. Gotta admit though you had a flair, a real flourish, the way you handled yourself. If I could've put the squeeze on you then I woulda, but I was already a couple quarts low."

He starts tightening his fingers a bit, putting the pressure on. "Why'd you wait so long to show up here?" I asked him.

"Had some other things on my mind I had to handle first."

"I know the feeling."

"Seems like you would, seein' as how you appear to be a might out of your noggin'."

"Now that's just insulting."

The rain intensifies. Thunder erupts above us, swarming over the house and breaking savagely across the yard. Sheet lightning slashes down like white-hot razor wire, shearing off tree limbs and leaving fires scattered among the tree line. Herbie starts getting a touch nervous, gritting his teeth and watching the flames writhing in the storm. A chuckle works loose in my chest. I ask, "So, did Johnny bring you or did you bring him?"

"Who the hell's Johnny?"

"The boy you strangled. Claimed he was your son, remember? I saw you talking to him out on the lawn before, laughing together. What did he say to you? He gonna keep coming back here?"

Herbie's got to raise his voice over the wind and fierce rain. "One thing's for certain, boy, you're crazier than three cats in a dryer."

"Coming from you that's a laugh."

"Maybe so. Say goodbye to this sorry world."

He's waited too long though. His crutches have sunk and slipped in the mud and slowly shifted to the left. His grip has loosened without him even knowing it. I break hard to one side and throw a fist at his face as hard as I can. It catches him on the temple, but he hardly notices.

The rain can't cool the heat inside my head anymore. "You've got accounts to settle, Herbie. Johnny wants his fair share of justice, and that's why he's brought you to me."

Those teeth shine the darkness again. "That so?"

"Come on, put the squeeze on me."

"You left me to die, son. I reckon that to be a might un-neighborly."

"You're a killer of children."

"Some, it's true. But that's my mission."

My mother's song remains behind in the air like the scent of jasmine. Her soft voice drifts through the brush. It confounds Herbie too, who keeps glancing around. "What is that?"

"I'm your savior," I tell him.

"What's that?"

I get my hands on his shirt collar, but he flings me from him easily. The cloth tears in my hands and the muscles ripple on his heavy arms, that mighty, massive chest swelling as he takes another deep breath.

"You need more heroes like me in this here world,

someone of distinguished valor and admirable exploits, that's what it is."

If he recognizes his own words now, he doesn't show it. "That right?"

"I'm gonna make my mama proud today."

"Only if she's gonna be proud to see you dead."

"Let's find out."

"I don't believe you quite understand the situation we got here, boy."

"And I believe I do."

He comes forward with his shoulders low, bulling his way into me. His eyes have a chummy light playing in them. Brake lights on the roadside. We hit, grunting, shoulder-to-shoulder. He has a lot more weight behind him, and the ground is too wet and slippery for my bare feet to dig in. I slide back and nearly go over. He slams into me again, charging on the crutches, and the handles come together hard on my collarbone. It hurts and a red blaze fills my head as we cling together and grapple. I drive hard into his barrel-chest and he laughs in my face. To him I'm seven years old and all he wants to do is get his fingers around my throat.

I reach out and seize him by the neck. I try to strangle him exactly as he's choking me, but I don't have the upper body strength Herbie does. It's not going to work like this. Already there's a blazing nimbus of yellow spots in my vision. He's having fun, really getting into it now, throttling me and yanking me side to side. I thrust my hand down and miss, try again and manage to grab hold of his pinned up pant leg. It takes a hell of a lot of finagling but Herbie's still in no rush to kill me outright, so I have some time. The spots grow larger, bubbling. He's enjoying the noises I make as he jerks me back and forth—"Whagh, whoogh, yeack."

I manage to shred the loose cloth and pull it from him. It's wet and heavy and I twirl it around until it feels thick as rope. I loop it around his neck and haul for whatever I'm worth. It doesn't do much besides throw him off balance a little, which is enough for me to break loose. I fall back into palmetto and cypress and lay in the mud coughing, gasping.

Rain comes down so violently that I feel like I'm underwater. Burning ozone fills my head and my flesh is alive and crawling off my bones. Herbie looks pretty hysterical with his hair and beard electrified, sticking out on end and dancing with blue static. The charge in the air quickly grows heavier, intolerable.

I look up at the window and see the fists of my brothers pressed against the glass. A soft hand touches my shoulder and suddenly yanks me backwards.

Someone's feet are off to one side, sticking out of the brush.

A pair of boots jutting from beneath the brush. I recognize them immediately. They're size twelve.

They're my fathers.

The phone is ringing. The voices gnaw at the back of my brain. Herbie crutches his way forward after me again, still grinning, sparks shooting out of his hair. The lightning arrives between us in one blinding, insane moment as the storm of ghosts blasts its all-embracing fury into my heart.

IN my mother's dreams she's following my father through the ironwood and swamp cyrilla into the deep slough of the bayou. The perfume of magnolia and sweet gum fills her head as a fog rolls across the morass, covering snapping turtles and noisy heron. She places her feet carefully, unlike my father who's rushing and plowing through the palmetto.

His face is so tight that it looks as if the flesh of his cheekbones will rip along its creases. His camera snaps against his chest so hard that surely the lens will crack at any moment. He's out of breath and hissing through his teeth as if he's in great pain. He stumbles, goes to one knee and curses, gets up but trips again immediately, falling to the other knee.

The swamp remains his enemy, even now. He's tried to kill and drain it off but despite all his efforts he hasn't disturbed a full inch of it. The heavy machinery fights the entire day long, dozens of men harrowing, smoothing and bulldozing, and yet each new morning they find themselves in exactly the same place. The loons laugh. My father laughs too, wearily, his boots covered in the slime of ages.

Now he's running—scampering, really—as the afternoon turns to purple and stars peer out of the east. My mother easily glides among the poplar trees while he gashes his arms on branches. His blood dapples bark and leaves, ripped pieces of his shirt hanging on barbs and thorns. He's a man obsessed by all that attracts him. And all that attracts him is everything that dooms him.

He stops to light a cigarette but his hands are trembling so badly that he can't get his lighter to work. When he finally manages a flame he brings the lighter to his mouth so quickly that he knocks the cigarette from his lips. It falls into the mud and the mist claws at his legs.

Someone else watching him might think he was lost,

but he clearly has a destination in mind. He might despise the bayou but he knows it intimately, much better than it appears. He acts like a hunted animal as my mother follows. She plucks an orchid and places it in her hair. Every so often she jams her knuckles into her mouth to suppress her misery. She isn't trying to hide but my father never bothers to look behind at where he's been or what harm he's caused along the way. His narrow vision is what puts him at odds with all that comprises his world, but he never thinks of leaving. He doesn't believe he can alter his course, so never does.

My mother recognizes the place and so do I. He's trampled miles of cabbage palm leading to the flat rock. This doesn't surprise her, or me either. He's always been plagued by the site and its significance and age, the profane antiquity of the rock. It sometimes keeps him awake at night, knowing that Kingdom Come is forever entwined with the ancient history of seeping ground and stone he cannot move.

I've begun to suspect, now, who he might be meeting here, though my mother still doesn't know. I tell her to go. I shout for her to leave this place, but she remains hunched among the cypress, the orchid standing out in its magnificent color amidst the green.

In these dreams there's a hint of a smile upon her sad face, the slightest touch of fear. Her fingernails trail in the fog, swirling it like river water. This is a time of revelation for all involved. My stomach tightens, the sweat runs into my mouth. He eases his camera to his eye, pointing, panting, aiming, because he doesn't want to miss an instant of this.

"Mama, go," I urge, and her hand rises from the mist as if to quiet me.

We watch as my wife Maggie walks towards my father, smiling for his camera and for him. My mother's face drops in on itself, every plane and angle breaking into pieces.

In my mother's dreams I say, "Mama, don't look anymore," and she tells me, "Oh, Thomas, it's much too late for that."

JOHNNY, the murdered boy, is giving me mouth to mouth, breathing bugs and bilge into my lungs.

I can barely see with a fiery afterimage glare cutting across my vision, but Johnny Jonstone's right in my face. His gray eyes are thankful yet beseeching, and he's thumping on my chest with his dead little fists. I taste mosquitoes under my tongue. His flesh is cold but the fever in my forehead is drilling even deeper. I'm on my back in a tremendous puddle, nearly going under, but he's got my chin tilted back and my nostrils pinched off, his lips sealed over mine.

He smiles when he sees I'm alive and awake and mouths something I can't understand. I roll aside, take a long drink of the dirty water and vomit until there's nothing left to give but bile. I keep retching and my stomach feels like it's about to squeeze out between my ribs. I try to stand several times and finally make it to my feet. The rain lashes my bare back and, being a proper penitent, I almost enjoy the punishment.

Herbie's still on fire.

His corpse hisses and spits where the drops touch his blackened skin and blazing clothes. The flooded grass beneath him has boiled and burned away and the mud's dried hard as cement. His crutches are stuck four inches deep in it and his body slumps and hangs there in the wind, spewing yellow gobs of bubbling fat. The flames swirl, lick and devour, filling him, rising from his open mouth. His pretty teeth are charcoal now. He'll grin all the way to hell and then some.

Johnny's gone. So are my father's shoes.

I leave Herbie burning and head back to the house. My legs barely respond and I'm forced to shuffle and lumber forward, falling a lot and clambering back up. I look to my brothers' window to see if they're laughing at me, but the room is utterly dark. I'm spastic and the shaking gets so bad that I'm afraid my shoulders will pop out of their sockets.

The phone is ringing. I manage to swing open the back door and plod into the kitchen. I grab the receiver and the buzzing of my brothers' angry voices spouts across the room.

I growl into the mouthpiece, "Whine all you want to, I'm still alive and I'll be seeing you in a minute."

I gently hang up the phone and head for the stairs, but I'm so exhausted that I crumple on the fifth step and tumble back down to the ground floor. I crash on my face. The fillings in my back teeth have melted and run. When I close my jaw my whole head chimes faintly.

At last I've made enough noise to awaken Dodi and she rushes to me wearing only one of my T-shirts and a pair of lace panties. "Oh God amighty, Thomas, what's happened to you! You're all burnt!"

"I—"

"You went outside tonight, didn't you, even thought I told you that only the real badness was comin' for us!" For the first time I see her mother in her, all of Velma Coots' hard line attitude showing through. "But you had to just go on anyway, without a thought in your whole big brain. Damn, I'll get some salve for your chest and neck. Most of your hair's gone too!"

"Help me up."

"You never do listen to all the good advice that folks try to give you. Headstrong, that's what you are. Mulish. Mama says it too. This ain't the way you set about to savin' the people of this town like you're supposed to! You're just set in your ways and stubborn that you won't listen to anything anybody else has to say no matter how smart it is. Why, I think that—"

"Dodi, shut up and help me over to the divan."

"I'm callin' Doc Jenkins."

I try to nod but my head tips the wrong way. "Him and the sheriff both. Go on now."

She drags me to the sofa, runs off for a minute and comes back with some foul ointment she daubs all over me. It makes my eyes tear but she keeps smearing it on. "Why you want the sheriff?"

"Just do it."

"Baby Jesus in the manger, I ain't never seen burns like these before. Even your eyebrows are near gone. The hell happened? Was you outside in the rain? Was you hit by lightnin'?"

"Pretty damn close."

She snorts and strands of her hair flap from the corners of her mouth. "It's a miracle you ain't dead."

"Call Doc Jenkins, Dodi."

"Oh, tha's right."

She runs to the kitchen while I lie there quivering and jerking, teeth ringing and the stench of the balm jockeying to trade places with the stink of ozone and fried flesh. The walls warp out of shape and close in. I get the dry heaves but they fade fast. There's not an ounce left in me to give.

"Storm's knocked the phone out," she says. "It's just makin' an awful racket and I can't get a dial tone."

"Put some clothes on," I tell her. "Take the truck, go into town and get them to come out here."

"No way am I drivin' in this weather!" she squeals. "You jest got done bein' struck by lightnin' and now you want me to go out there? The hell is that? Ain't you got no concern for my well bein'?"

"You'll be fine."

"That's easy for you to say. Lightnin' ain't gonna hit you twice tonight. Skip right over you and nail me instead."

She isn't going to do it unless I somehow make her feel safe. That's exceedingly difficult to do lying here crisped and twitching. "It's my storm of souls, Dodi, not yours. It's here for me. Nobody else is going to get hurt right now. Go get Doc and Sheriff Burke."

"Mama," she says. "I should go tell her what's happened. Maybe Mama can do the proper thing for you."

"Not at this second. For right now I need you to— "

"Okay, hush, I'll go."

She makes me as comfortable as possible on the divan and puts a sheet over me that sticks to the salve and oozing burns. She throws on a wind-breaker, takes my keys and goes without another word.

I look up the stairway at the closed door to my brothers' bedroom.

The house breathes its extensive history. A century ago the dead were laid out in this same room and shown in their coffins for three days of mourning. My forefathers rested here through the long nights. I keep waiting for Johnny to start tapping at the screen again but he doesn't. He's served his purpose, whatever it might be. I hope to Christ that Herbie's leg doesn't come looking for me. I've had just about enough of those two.

Dodi's stuck in the mud. The tires of the truck scream but she doesn't engage the four-wheel drive. Gravel, silt and muck spatter the front windows as the rain continues to thrash against the glass. Shifting from reverse directly into third gear, back and forth, she finally manages to grind and rock the truck loose. Hopefully the transmission won't fall out before she hits town.

The burns are beginning to hurt. I've done my best not to look down and inspect myself but as I quiver the sheet rubs harshly against the raw places. I run my fingers through my hair feeling how short and well-trimmed it is now. The ridges of my brows are tender.

Rooms mutter with the extent of the past. The wind stamps its foot on the roof and the rafters groan as if about to buckle beneath the weight of the black sky. We're alone. The poetry is gone but our responsibilities to blood remain. I've an apology to make to Jonah. I never should've urged Sarah to leave, no matter what the consequences. It wasn't my place to save anyone from the impossibility of the commonplace. They deserved the chance to fail, no more or less than anybody.

I toss the sheet off and move, in spasms, up the stairs. Whatever my brothers have brought upon me they've brought upon themselves, and we'll face it together. It's the promise I made to my parents so long ago.

Our hate is only another part of our love. Perhaps

we'll survive it and perhaps we won't. There are no guarantees anymore, if there ever were. We're all unprotected now. The house voices its concern, moaning, wind in the attic and the dampness bloating the timbers. Maybe someone stalks the second and third floors, carrying a reap hook or a camera.

It could be. But I'm more concerned with my missing eyebrows. The ridge of my frontal lobe feels huge and significant. I catch a glimpse of my reflection in the window and know I could easily substitute for any of my brothers now. I've been redesigned to snap into the proper place.

With each step I take the pain in my side grows greater. It's as if Sebastian is still biting me, tearing through my flesh so that our sister can be born. Her face, body, and following that, her name. What do they call her up there in the shadows, tittering in the confines of that overwhelming brain? How am I supposed to address her?

Thunder pulses in a constant growl and the lightning shreds the night.

I reach the door.

It's unlocked.

I open it and enter, facing the darkness, full of my own rage and useless intent. Mulish. I turn on the light.

The bed sheets and covers are on the floor, balled in a corner like the makings of a nest. The windowpane is dirty with their fingerprints, but my brothers aren't here.

On the wall are words.

PENETRATION. ADD THIS TO YOUR TALLY OF DEFEATS BUT DO NOT SWAY FROM THE

COURSE. VALUE SHORTCOMINGS. MEANING. THE MIND IS DISSATISFIED WITH THE SEXUAL URGE AND THE LIBIDO FINDS NO MERIT IN THE BASAL GANGLIA. SIGNIFI-CANCE. IRRATIONAL NUMBERS AND THEIR DECIMAL EXPANSIONS ARE NECESSARILY NONTERMINATING AND NONPERIODIC. THE HAM IS STILL IN THE HOUSE.

CHAPTER ELEVEN

DOC Jenkins pulls up my eyelids, shines his penlight in and says, "Aspirin will help with the pain, a bit. That salve is good for the burns so leave it on even if it does smell like a New Orleans whorehouse at low tide. As for that shaking, it'll stop eventually." He wags his head. "Or maybe it won't. Nothing to be done about it. You survived. Most don't, so be grateful. Drink lots of fluids. Read your bible. Oh, and no sex for at least a couple of days. See the dentist soon and have those fillings replaced. You want to go to a hospital?"

"No."

"Didn't think so."

Doc is built low to the ground, stocky with especially long hominoid arms, hairy knuckles, gray wiry thatches on his ears thick as scouring pads. He doesn't wear bow ties but there must be some kind of an optical illusion at work because I always think he's got one on, I can see it. He's wearing a pleated vest and a pocket watch with a fob made of sallow curls. His paunch bounces a little as he swings around the room, and he might be considered a jolly-looking little man if only he ever smiled.

"What about Herbie?" I ask.

"That the crispy critter? No amount of fluids or sex is gonna help him much now. That motherless son has been charred down to a burnt match stick."

Lips crawling, Burke makes faces. He's out of his element and under pressure here in my home. He's still got his anger and frustration prodding him along but he's trying to show a certain amount of reverence for my grandfather, whom he respected and feared as a boy, and my family history. I figure he'll return to his natural belligerency pretty soon, and I want to get as much information out of him as I can before it happens.

He won't take his hat off inside. He needs those stately inches, even with me down on the couch with no eyebrows. "I ran a check on that name you gave me. If this really is Herbie Jonstone then he's a pretty bad prick. Got out of Angola a few weeks back and he's already wanted for knocking over four convenience stores between here and Mississippi. Has three cases of sodomy stacked up on him, possible murder charges. A few of his former associates and their families have gone missing."

"He dumps them in the swamp."

The sheriff's chin first juts one way and then the other. Burke is tonguing the empty spaces where his back teeth used to be. If he doesn't get a couple of bridges made soon his cheeks will start to sink in. "Why was this convict in Kingdom Come? What brought him here on such a straight run?"

A few last flashes of lightning close up and fiery, illuminating the property. The deputies are in the back trying to work Herbie onto a stretcher, but he keeps crumbling like cigarette ash whenever they grab him too hard. The storm, having made its point, now withdraws and sinks into the background. Thunder continues to rumble in the distance, a smug and steady presence.

"To finish something he left unfinished a long time ago."

"You knew him?"

"You could say so."

Burke's nasty tiny eyes fill with all sorts of abstractions as he runs various possibilities through his head: me and Herbie were partners, maybe I've got a network of hit men working for me, that's where the money comes from, all those convenience store robberies—he wants to sucker me into a trap but has no clue how to do it and settles for just looking at me suspiciously.

"He tried to kill me in the bayou when I was a kid," I tell him.

"What? The hell you say. Why isn't that in our records?"

"I never told anyone. I thought a bull gator had gotten him."

Doc scratches his earlobe and gets his finger tangled. "A piece of him anyway. Had no left leg below the knee."

Burke's voice wavers again in his excitement and skips up to the next octave. "So he comes here after twenty years to finish doing you in, the two of you tussle in the yard, and he winds up being struck by lightning? That the long and short of this story?"

It seems as if there should be a lot more to it, but I don't know what else there might be. "Yeah, that just about covers it all."

"You must've pissed the man off pretty good. First thing he does when he gets off the Farm is come lookin' for you. Guess you knew how to stir up trouble and get under somebody's skin even when you was a boy."

"He's a child murderer. It didn't take much."

"I reckon not."

I'm fading fast and keep catching myself beginning to nod. The pain settles in further and really starts to bite. Dodi says, "You're gettin' pale, Thomas. I think it'd be best if you got some sleep now." She smears more of the salve across my chest, and her hands make me hum. She's still only wearing my T-shirt and lace panties. She wiggles to the kitchen and returns with a glass of water and five aspirin. I swallow them all but can't get more than a sip of water down.

"For Christ's sake girl," Burke bellows, "go put some clothes on. It ain't decent you walkin' all over creation with hardly anything on your body. Didn't your mama teach you nothin' right?"

"Plenty," Dodi says.

"I got a few more questions," he says to me.

"Sure," I tell him. "Just don't ask anything about my vinegar."

"Vinegar? Why you talkin' about vinegar? Doc, his brains fried up like grits and eggs, and he was never too clever to begin with."

But Doc enjoys staring at Dodi and now he's irritated that Burke has sent her away to cover herself up. One hand holds his black bag and the other lengthy arm dangles and as if he might bring it up to club the sheriff.

The deputies have tossed Herbie in the back of

Doc's wagon, and they have to borrow a hammer to break up the hardened earth to free the crutches. Herbie Jonstone has mostly boiled out from the inside. He's hardly more than cinders, but I'm surprised that enough of his face is intact that I can still recognize him. His lips are gone so he's got even more of his smile to show.

"Looks like the good Lord had something to say about that old boy," Burke says, and I can hear the laughter beginning to bubble in his voice. I glance up into his eyes and listen to the clock tick off the seconds until the other shoe drops—one, two, three, Burke getting his leer nice and right on his face, four, and there it is coming 'round the curve, five— "And about you too."

His smirk isn't that much different from Herbie Jonstone's, and it makes me think of the tally of my defeats, the value of shortcomings, and where the ham might be if it's really in the house.

IN my mother's nightmare she is about to be murdered.

It starts with the stink of stale smoke and sour beer. She's drinking tequila in Leadbetter's while the men play darts to see who'll get to take her out into the parking lot. The animal heads peer down at my mama and several times over the passage of the night she talks aloud to them, laughing, climbing up onto the bar stool so she can kiss them on their dusty snouts.

A guy named Willy plugs the number twenty on the board and then follows it with a bull's eye. His whole life is scrawled across his face, down to the smallest detail. You can read his thoughts as they rattle and clang together in his cluttered brain. He works at the mill and he's eager to take his jealousy and frustrations out on the boss's wife. He grabs my mother's forearm and hauls her out to his truck, tosses her in and then lunges forward to kiss her. Willy hasn't got much in the way of finesse.

He fumbles at her blouse and pops off a button that arches onto the dashboard. He groans harshly, a beast that's been kicked almost to death, which is pretty much what he is. He tries to dry hump her leg but the gear shift blocks him and he winds up rubbing against that for a while, hardly noticing the difference. Willy is what you might call a single-track individual. Moonlight descends through the passenger window and outlines my mother in flaming mercury.

Beneath Willy's lips she is laughing. It's a grisly, unnatural sound that presses ice to Willy's spine and makes him pull back. He stares at her, so beautiful there with this unsettling noise coming up out of her throat. Maybe she needs to throw up. He's not unfeeling, this particular Willy. He pats her arm like a good friend and tries to shove her out the door so that she doesn't fuck up his floor mats.

Still, he really wants a piece of ass but now he's thinking about how it looks. He's already been written up three times on the job and it would probably be considered excessively stupid in the way of financial planning if he's caught with the boss's wife. No wonder the guys all looked a little relieved when they didn't win that goddamn dart game. Linnigan and Tyrell both definitely shanked on the nineteen.

What happens if she screams rape? His pecker runs for cover and takes a downturn against his thigh. He thinks about physical evidence and glances around.

Shit, the button, where the hell's the button gone? She's still laughing quietly but at least she hasn't gotten sick yet.

"Uh," Willy says, "hey, listen, I think that maybe we've got, uhm, like a misunderstanding here, you know." He curses the dart board his wife got him for Christmas that's hung up out in the garage. He puts in a couple hours of practice every night out there, getting the proper wrist action down. Damn the bitch, why couldn't she have bought him the new socket wrenches he'd asked for? But no, fuck no.

Broadhead skinks skitter through the gutter. My mother leans forward now, bewitching, enticing, getting him roused again, sort of, her breath coming in short bursts. She's nearly hyperventilating. The windows fog quickly and beads of precipitation run down the windshield.

The flashing neon beer signs cast a nimbus through the haze. Her hands reach out, all talon and bone, and Willy whines partly out of lust and the rest from fright. She's still giggling, much more softly and quietly, muttering to herself, a woman in pain. Willy can't make out the words but since she's talking he figures he'll join in the conversation, see where it goes.

"You're so pretty, I mean, more than that really, I've always watched you, thought about you, I mean, we all have. What else are we gonna do, right? It's only natural, that, us watching, I'm sure you ain't gonna hold a grudge about it, am I right? But it's not—it's not safe for a woman like you to be out at a place like this, so late at night, flashing your gams, titties shaking, you need a touch more support there, in my opinion. My wife, her bras are these pointy torpedo lookin' things, lots of wire, them Winnebagos ain't never gonna droop. And there you are climbing onto bar stools and kissing decapitated animal heads and such, might be some talk about that around town, you know. You might wanna forego such activities, at least this close to home."

She likes his voice apparently and closes her eyes to listen to him spout. It goes on for a while longer, some stammering here and there but not too much, with Willy unsure of exactly how this damn scene is going to play out. If any of the guys are watching maybe he can send a signal, write something on the fogged up windshield—HEY, I GOT A SITUATION HERE, COME FUCKING HELP ME OUT—but he'd have to write it backwards and he's not too sure how many of them guys can read anyway.

Her blouse is open another button and her skirt is hiked to almost mid-thigh. That mouth is glowing gray in the dim light, laced with neon crimson ever few seconds as the signs flash, lips growing more and more wet as the tip of her tongue prods along the edges.

Willy decides to just go through with it. His wife isn't doing much for him after having three kids in two and a half years, and she lets the oldest one sleep in bed between them, like a chocolate- and shit-smudged buffer. As if that's not bad enough, Willy isn't allowed to watch TV anymore.

When his wife isn't planted in front of the tube watching soaps or talk shows the kid is glued to the carpet about six inches from the screen, still using the remote to change channels about every ten seconds. It makes Willy nuts and drives him out of the house and into the garage where he throws darts until he can feel the capillaries in the recesses of his heart about to rupture. His brother Jackson had been only three years older than him and was already dead from a myo-cardial infarction. Jackson had gotten a treadmill for Christmas, went out and bought himself a warm-up suit, new tennis shoes, sweatbands, water bottle, head-phones so he could listen to the soundtrack to "Chari-ots of Fire," took about eleven steps on the thing and fell over dead. Ever since Willy had seen his brother with painted pink cheeks in his casket he'd just been counting down the days until it was his turn.

My mother presses her palm flat against Willy's chest and pushes slightly, a go-on-geddouta-here ges-ture, as if they're long-time friends. It takes him a minute to see that she's got tears on her cheeks even though she's not really sobbing. It gets him thinking about the cops again and the dime bag of weed he's got stashed under the back seat. He wonders why he didn't think this whole thing through a little better, why he didn't back the fuck off when he saw her nuz-zling the wild boar's dead head. He should be able to put one and one together by now but he never does.

He tries again, unsure of how to proceed. He wants to just get it done and go get a beer, wait for the depu-ties to come drag him out by his ankles. "Ah, see, it's like this if you wanna know the truth, my job gets me down some, nothin' against your husband a'course, and my house, well it's a wreck and there's all this noise, screaming all the time and there's candy bar wrappers on the floor, and the babies, Jesus, she doesn't know how to feed them, half the food's in their hair for Christ's sake. So that's why I need to, you know, to look at somebody like you, it's why the guys stare, the fact that you're so beautiful. That and, well, you gettin' up on the stool and all. It's why I want the sex. With you. In case you were speculatin'."

She doesn't bother to pull her blouse together as she turns in her seat to open the passenger door. Willy almost reaches out to stop her but he's stuck on the gear shift again and is starting to prefer it. Moonlight blazes in around her so brightly that Willy has to avert his eyes. She closes the truck door and walks across Leadbetter's parking lot to the brush while Willy grunts with relief and decides he'll tell his buddies he finished the deed with the boss's wife. He won't have to say much seeing as how they won't believe him anyway, all of them having failed in this before as well.

My mother looks down and sees a pair of boots.

I know them too. They're my father's.

And the hands around her neck, caressing at first and then tightening, they're his too.

THE Crone has somehow gotten into the house again. I wake up in my—my brothers'—bedroom and she's standing there staring at the wall of words.

It's still dark out. She moves her toothless mouth when she reads, plucking at her lengthy chin hairs, cocking her head and repeating phrases. The words have been carefully carved in using an old-fashioned key, which was left sticking out of the plaster at the bottom of the last letter. She grunts and runs her bony finger along the grooves and curves.

"Does it mean anything to you?" I ask.

She takes a breath that sounds as if it might never stop rattling around in her chest. Her brittle voice rustles, crackles and ticks. "Hell no...you'd have to be out of your head for this fool talk to make sense." She gums more of the words and swallows them down. "What's this here? This basal ganglee?"

I sit up and the raw skin pulling makes me champ at my tongue. It takes a few seconds for the pain to subside enough for my vision to clear. Sheets are covered in ointment and soot but not much blood. I lean back against the headboard and light a cigarette. "Nerves deep in the brain."

"Well, they'd be the right boys to talk about such things I suppose. Where are they?"

I struggle not to hiss. "I don't know."

"How'd they get there?"

"No idea."

"You miss 'em?"

It's an average question, a common one, and perhaps it's the normality of it that takes me back. I hadn't thought of it in terms like this. Missing them implies love, or at least affection, and we are somehow beyond that, being blood. She knows this but is testing me. We've still got a long way to go before we get to the heart of the matter, if we ever do.

"Where's that Coots girl?"

"Upstairs. She's upset that my brothers are gone."

"Here, let me bum a butt."

I offer her a cigarette and give her a light. She inhales deeply and the eras that have worn down her shrunken frame seem to flash by. She is dainty, she is young, she's refined and smokes like a noblewoman. She's dancing with my great-grandfather and laughing at his feeble attempts at romance. I can imagine her doing a two-step shuffle around the room with bits and tatters coming off her as she sways until there's nothing left of her except a small pile of rags.

Those charms and bells sewn into her filthy clothing ring in time with my melted fillings, chiming through the house and my head.

She sits on the end of their bed, somewhat uneasy. The nest of sheets and blankets on the floor in the corner seems as if it should have huge eggs laid within it. "Looks like you had yourself a hurtful night," she says, gesturing to my wounds. "The storm do that to you?"

I have to think about it before I answer. "Mostly it was a killer named Herbie, who felt compelled to come back here to the bayou. Considering he survived a bull gator attack many years back, he probably felt invincible in the bottoms. He was finished off by lightning."

"Really?" the Crone asks, blowing smoke in a thin billow. "Hmph, you got more good luck floating about you than anybody I ever knowed. More ghosts and puzzles too."

That's twice she's told me that and it's starting to get to me a little. I look from her to the words and back again. "Why?" I ask, genuinely curious. "Why do you think that is?"

"Some questions ain't worth askin'."

"And some are."

Her face is stark but not hollow. There's an energy in those wrinkles that means something I'll never understand. She carries a thousand epitaphs that won't ever fully convey her life's signature.

"You even got yourself a nice haircut out of it," she says.

I run my hand through my shortened curls again, and it's true, I sort of like it.

"Guess that's one secret that don't have you no more. This bad fella from the past."

"No, not any longer. But another has been eating at me. Who killed my grandmother on the roof of the school?"

She waves the question off. "Nobody knows that and nobody ever will, I'm thinkin'. You won't find all the answers no matter how hard you try."

"Probably not," I agree. "So what are you here for?"

"I done told you once, I got to reserve my consternation for the right time and the proper folks."

"This the time?"

"No."

She finishes the cigarette, wets her fingertips with her tongue and puts out the burning ember. She carefully conceals the filter somewhere in her tatters, possibly to use in a spell somewhere down the line. Settling herself on the mattress she lets out a relieved sigh and begins to drop off. The silence of the house is compelling and relaxing. It can be an overwhelming influence of serenity and solace. I wonder if I should put her to bed in one of the other rooms.

Wavering a bit as the dust settles around her, she takes in the quiet. "At least your brother isn't crying his blues anymore."

"Not here anyway."

"Not anywhere. He's got himself a new way to grieve."

"What is it?"

She shrugs and her rags slip across her shoulders. "You got any more of that pound cake?"

"No," I say, "but I could make another if you like. It won't take long."

"Nah, don't go to no bother. I just had a hankering for it."

We're about done for the night and I can feel her gathering her resolve to leave. Sometimes it can be difficult, with the night and the darkness and quiet pressing down and the smell of sweetgum settling in. "Last time you were here you were talking about the past."

"Yep."

"About how it can die and be reborn."

"I got's to get going."

She gets up and shuffles out of the room, but pauses at the doorway. I give it a three count as she stands there, waiting, and then ask, "Did you dance with my great-grandfather?"

"That man owned two left feet and thirteen arms. Had me a hell of a time fighting him off. Few men take no for an answer, and he sure wasn't one of 'em. Had to use tooth and claw to pertect my virginity." She glances back, reading the shadows lying across me and says, "Drink some oxtail soup, it's good for you."

"Fuck no."

A childlike titter breaks free from the cobwebs far inside her body as she leaves and shuts the door. I hear her hobbling steps all the way down the stairs and out across the front yard into the greater darkness. The willows brush against the shingles as if pleading with me to call her back.

I do miss my brothers, and they are singing a new brand of blues. I can feel the song occasionally prodding the back of my head and every so often my side erupts with agony. Retribution is waiting for us all. I've checked the house for them and now Dodi is in another bedroom surviving her guilt because she feels she'd somehow failed in her duties to them. I listened to her weeping earlier, surprised that she'd taken their leaving so deeply to heart.

I take the key off the night stand and hold it clasped

in my fist. It must fit somewhere even if nothing else does.

Maybe they followed Johnny Jonstone back into the swamp.

There's only one way to find out.

Tomorrow I'll head into the bayou.

THE ham is still in the house.

I've got the key and I try it in every lock I can think of even when I know it's not going to fit. Every bedroom, closet, storage area, and bathroom door. I spend an hour in my parents' bedroom going through belongings I've never touched before. My mother's jewelry chests, cabinets, dresser drawers, desk compartments, anything at all with a lock no matter how undistinguished. I enter rooms I haven't stepped foot in since I was a child. I'm surprised at how clean everything is. Dodi has really kept the place up.

She sleeps curled around pillows. She's wept herself into exhaustion. I stand over her, wanting to make love and not wanting to make love, yet hoping she'll awaken. The Crone has gotten me into the mood to talk, but except for an occasional grimace Dodi appears to sleep deeply and peacefully enough. I lay beside her for a while enjoying the company.

She'll be leaving soon, I know, now that my brothers are gone. I take her hand and press my lips to her palm, brushing her knuckles across my cheek. I hope to Christ she doesn't start hacking off her fingers too.

I leave her and close the door quietly behind me, heading up to the attic.

There's a century of packed, hidden and lost effects up here. Dozens of knotted lives and deaths

drifting through time. There's nowhere to start looking because each inch and article is only another chapter of somebody's continuing existence. Their mem-
oirs and confessions and endless guilt. There are fifty
broken arms packed beneath the rafters. Twenty abortions, sixteen rapes, a couple kidnappings, four mur-
ders, a thousand clandestine affairs and shrouds of
indemnity. Innumerable veiled threats and countless
failures.

Niches, cubbyholes, and crawlspaces abound
stuffed with boxes, furniture, trunks, furnishings, toys,
possessions and personal effects beyond my understanding. I pick up a thin polished piece of wood with
two metal clasps and a pointed end set against a spring.
I could stare at it for the rest of my life and never
learn its intent. But it's not junk, nothing here is. All
of it has a meaning and reason even if it's never known
again.

This is family.

There are locks upon locks.

Dozens, perhaps hundreds of them. We must've
been a secretive people once, carefully preserving, protecting and placing our items away in the time before
the secrets owned us. So much to be hidden and safeguarded and secured. The shadows were made for just
such things, and these things were made for the shadows. I shouldn't be here because I haven't brought
anything to leave behind. This is a sacred place of
ancestry and kindred history, and I can feel the im-
portance of what has been harbored in the house.

The storm of ghosts hasn't done much to shake
loose any of the dead. They're still snug and cozy and
quiet. I want to start calling out names—"Grandfather? Uncle Jonathan? Aunt Fidencia? Rollie! Nicole!

Jort?"—but there are too many for me to remember.

The key fits many of the locks but won't turn once inside them. For a moment I wonder if the mechanisms have been rusted shut or jammed with lost years. But if that were true my brothers wouldn't have left the key for me. I can see their shambling tri-fold form moving carefully among the contents of the attic, crooked and gnarled and toiling, just to spray a drop of oil into a lock so that one day I might find whatever needs to be found.

They have been put in charge of this as I was put in charge of them. Why did they give it up now? Is it a sign of trust? Or will I be unlocking the box of my own undoing?

For hours I walk among the remnants, chronicles and accounts of my family, hunting. I think about how the mind might actually be dissatisfied with the sexual urge, and how irrational numbers are necessarily nonterminating and nonperiodic.

We are archaic. We are tuned to the deceased, and still my brothers' blues thrum through my basal ganglia with rhythm and skill.

Just before dawn, as the light streams in through the single attic window, I find the lock that the key fits.

Penetration.

It's an old black trunk covered with stamps and stickers from foreign cities that looks as if it's been around the world twice before returning to Kingdom Come. The key slides in and turns easily, perfectly, the hard snap of metal on metal extremely loud in the silence of this crypt.

I ease the hasp down and open the trunk.

My mother lies within, wrapped in clear plastic,

shrunken and contorted as any of my brothers. She smiles in her rictus and remains exactly as my father has left her: dead but still dreaming.

And beneath her corpse, the wrapped body of a six-year-old kid. It's Johnny Jonstone.

CHAPTER TWELVE

CLAY the conjure boy, and his buddy Darr have their bikes parked outside of Doover's Five & Dime at around closing time when I pull up. There are dead cormorants, grebes, ring-neck ducks and heron scattered all around the area, some with their heads or wings missing. Whatever the brew is that they're cooking up takes a hell of a lot of bird parts. Mallards wallow across the Spanish moss and morass behind the store and snapping turtles hang off the skiff lines and traps draped in the mire.

Darr is the only one in sight. He's been raking up piles of feathers and bones with a threshing scoop, but now stops to withdraw his knife from a cormorant at his feet. He stomps on over, grinning like we're old buddies, cleaning his switchblade with a bandanna. There are stained croker sacks up on the porch that flutter, flop and roll a bit. This is getting a little out of hand.

His head is freshly shaven around the three strips of hair. Those jailhouse tattoos on his arms look larger and more intricate now, and I realize they're a work in progress. He, or perhaps Clay, has been adding to them with a needle and ink. The edges are a bright black and scabbing over, but I still can't make out what any of them are supposed to be.

He finishes wiping down the blade and replaces it in his right boot. The butterfly Band-Aid on his forehead has finally fallen off. "Back again?" he asks.

"I'm renting a skiff."

"Yeah, well now, that's good. Hey, you got yourself a nice haircut there."

"Thanks."

Clay steps out onto the porch and takes a seat on an old bench. He watches me carefully, expressionless but alert as always.

Darr says, "You know what I simply cannot stand?"

"Fencing," I answer.

"No, not fencing really, not in and of itself, as it goes," he tells me. "You see, seems like you've already forgotten."

"No, I haven't. You hate watching fencers who have no notion of the hardcore reality behind the art form. You've got to have convictions to live with the blade. Belief. But those players, they might as well be shooting hoops or sliding into third base. They never embrace the tenets and ideology behind that discipline."

"That's exactly correct, word for word!"

"It's a little trick I have."

That makes him laugh. He throws his head back and lets the guffaws loose and claps me on the back. "A damn good one, tossing people's words back at 'em."

Clay looks down at all the dead birds and a wrinkle crosses his features that might be embarrassment on anybody else. He still doesn't want any part of the ways of the granny witches but he's as caught up in the wheel as the rest of us. I step over to him and cock a thumb at Darr. "He's talking about fencing again."

"He can't help himself sometimes."

"You the one doing the tattoo work on him?"

"He does most of it with sewing needles. Lottie Mae touches it up some if need be."

I offer him a cigarette and he passes. Clay's got a look in his eyes like he's going to have to kill me one of these days although he's not quite sure why. Once again I get the feeling that he's been through something very much like this before. I want to ask him about it.

"You've come again," he says, "to bother my sister."

"No, I'm here to rent a skiff."

"Why?"

"I need to find something in the bayou."

"What's that?"

"Maybe I'll explain it to you sometime."

We're still waiting for circumstances to play out in a specific fashion, the pattern growing larger until we can't see the threads of it anymore. The wingless grebes have something to do with the eyeless newts and the kicked dogs, my grandmother on the roof, my father in the mill, the flat rock, Eve's all day sucker.

I turn and head into the store but Lottie Mae is standing on the other side of the screen door just staring. I try to ignore her but it's impossible. It's obvious she's been busy lately.

She nudges the screen open with her hip and approaches with no trepidation at all. There's a scent of alcohol about her but it's not booze, it's rubbing alcohol. She's had her navel pierced and there's a very sharp tattoo on her belly. If Darr did this one too he's got a hell of a lot of talent. The design is something almost cabalistic but not exactly. Maybe it's a sign of protection or one of contrition.

At least she hasn't been downing any more vodka gimlets. She's dressed seductively and the air of confidence surrounding her makes her sultry in the extreme. She's had new training for her mission. The feathered points of her short dark hair are curled and wet with sweat, wisps clinging to her forehead. There's drama in her stance, the hint of misconduct and danger. Jesus, there's several swamp whores who can't cast sexuality with such a perfect aim. A gentle laugh flits from her throat and I know I'm the prey, and I like it.

"Lottie Mae?"

"Hello, Thomas, how are you?" She tilts towards me and gets a better look. "Oh my, what happened to you? Your eyebrows. And your neck, it's all burnt."

By now she and the whole town knows about Herbie the child killer, the storm of souls and my missing brothers. "I'm okay. I just came to rent a skiff from Doover."

"He ain't here today. I'm working the store."

"So long as I get a boat."

There's another, much uglier smell on her breath: it's oxtail soup. She's back to making incantations, perhaps now with her brother's help. Her resolve has returned along with a new sense of purpose.

She's completely split from the granny witches now. She's taken Clay's advice to stay away from the crazy old women and she finds herself much more capable without them. "You gonna stobpole into the bayou all on your lonesome? You ever done that before?"

"No."

"Then you'll be lost inside of ten minutes and nobody'll ever see you again. There's a thousand square miles of slough out there. How you gonna challenge that? A gator can take off the back end of a skiff with one bite or a swipe of the tail. Why you headin' into the swamp anyway?"

"Exercise. My doctor says I need to get out more."

"All Doc Jenkins knows is how to hand out aspirin and scratch his ole ugly ears. Skiff rental is five dollars for the afternoon. Some of them monastery folks come around on occasion, they want to go see the wonders of God out in the bayou, commune with nature. Usually Doover takes the charters out himself, if need be, but I can go with you instead."

She means it to be a temptation and it is. I can't understand why we're still at this. It's got nothing to do with the chants and hexes of the granny witches dancing around on my lawn in the rain. I'm not sure it's anything personal either. There's probably no reason anymore, we've simply become tangled up together and can't figure out a way to get free.

Her brother and Darr have been listening to our conversation.

"Heya," Darr says, "let's all go. I got nothing better to do for the rest of the day. We'll have a few beers, get to know one another a little more."

I'm still thinking of my brothers and Drabs and what else might be out there waiting for me in the bog. Snapping turtles cling and drop from the skiff lines, vanishing beneath the green ooze and mist writhing upon the water.

Clay stares at me.

"Sure," I tell them. "Sounds like fun."

SUNLIGHT skims off the cypress and tupelo trees, casting a fiery gleam against the woven layers of deep shadow. Crescent rows of dark shanties line the distant slopes of brush and morass, vine-draped and overgrown with hanging moss and orchids. A couple of doors clatter in the hot breeze of bog town. Faces appear pressed to the ramshackle pineboard slats, the glint off eyes and wet lips shining through the cracks in the rotting planks.

People have been dying out here by the hundreds since the beginning of the world, swallowed by the bayou without a ripple. Or they're found hanging among the sparkleberries after a week of being lost in the maze of green marsh, tormented by snakes, gators, and half-pound spiders. Potts County loses a half dozen almost every year, mostly adolescents who come out to conquer the bottoms.

Stobpoling takes a real finesse that I don't have. After lurching wildly for twenty minutes and almost tipping the boat several times, I let out a sigh and Clay rises. He takes the pole from me without a word and the skiff evens out immediately. He leads us through the stagnant water ways.

"Any particular direction?" he asks.

My grandmother's body had been impaled on the school roof facing west. For no other reason than that I say, "West."

"All right then."

Darr's got three six-packs in a chest of ice and already he's on his seventh or eighth beer. He hands me a can and I sit back and slowly drink it, enjoying the taste. This really is relaxing and almost feels like a camp-out with some friends. The company is good. A bull gator's powerful musk pervades the area, and it's not until we've been on the water for twenty minutes that I consider the possibility they've brought me out here to kill me.

An emerald wash of light ignites the side of Lottie Mae's ashen face, with a soft powdering of caramel-colored freckles standing out as if etched until she fairly glows in these shadows. She presses close across the seat as I shift away, her breath on my neck causing spasms in my groin. I have to stifle a groan. Clouds roll and snarl the sky as the sun chops down against tupelo and willow branches.

We pass more bog shanties that lean so far over they might fall into the bayou at any second. Pigs run wild in yards and there are tricycles upended in the shores of muck. Tupelo trees sway and waver along the slopes and leaves shake out over us. Boat motors growl nearby.

"We been orphaned since we were pretty young but the swamp takes care of its own," she says.

"What happened to your parents?"

"Mama got a fish bone wedged in her throat and died at the dinner table when I was eleven. Papa took a job hauling highly flammable materials but he never could quit smoking. Blew himself up one night outside of Memphis and it took them two days to put out of the flames."

I look towards Clay and he nods.

Darr finishes off a can of beer and tosses it over the side, where it plops and floats on the slime. "My daddy, he got caught burglarizing the house of the second cousin to the governor of Georgia. He would've made it too except he found some dirty magazines and took to reading them right there in the bedroom, all a'goggle. Guess it got his imagination rolling. The dumbass pervert didn't even hear the sirens when the sheriff pulled up. I did a deuce with Pa down in Jacksonville. Embarrassing, that's what it was. I mostly pretended I didn't know him."

I take the key to my mother's tomb out and toss it at the can. It rings loudly and both quickly sink.

"What was that?" Lottie Mae asks, and I hear a genuine curiosity and concern beneath the coquettish purr.

"Nothing important."

"Is anything important to you?"

"Yes."

"What?"

It's easy to say but hard to get across the meaning and intention. The word alone sounds foolish, but we'll go on from there. "Blood."

"Like in killing or like in kin?" She kicks her shoes off and I can see the catclaw briar scars and sycamore scratches that don't mar them in the least. The bright white orchids grow thicker the deeper we head into the swamp. Herons and loons follow us along the way, weeping.

Reflections flash in the distance, and the faint sounds of the calliope can be heard straining across the slough.

"Oh, listen," Lottie Mae says, "it's the carnival tonight. I forgot all about it."

It gets to me. "What?"

"Swamp folk put it together every year or two in the bottoms. Nothing fancy, just a get together, more or less. Big party, really. Some booths and stuffed toys. Sell hot dogs and frogs' legs. Got a couple of old rides they set up for the kids to go round in."

"I've never heard of it before," I say.

"You ain't from the bottoms."

"I got sick last year on that damn whirligig," Darr declares. "Thing's all rusted to shit with a gear box that sounds like it's packed with dirt. It was sorta fun before the getting sick part."

Clay the conjure boy, easy rider with uneasy eyes, holds my gaze tirelessly. He's barely sweating in the heat but the ropy veins stand out along his forearms and neck as he poles us along. He seems to be reading signs everywhere he looks—in each mound we pass, along every gator's back, and in each line of my face.

I smile and say, "Let's go."

DOZENS of skiffs float in the shallows, some tied to decaying docks, other fastened to branches of water elm or simply landed in the weeds. Drifting slowly in an eddy leading to a heap of bull grass, low out on a sand bank, we bump against the tiny island of morass. The titi shakes and waves as we go by. Clay swings the skiff in that direction and comes up to the tussock on the opposite side so we don't have to get our feet wet. The music is distant but loud, and Darr begins tapping his boot and humming along. Banjos, harmonicas and jug pipes carry on the rigid breeze. Clay is wary, taking everything in but rejecting its face value.

Lottie Mae's veneer is good but not perfect. From the corner of my eye I see her sexy pout occasionally droop with a quivering bottom lip. She's terrified. I scare the hell out of her but it's something more too.

I turn and tell her, "Don't worry."

The lip stiffens, her smile broadens. Body heat is turned up high and I try not to gulp air. I don't mind playing along and letting her spring whatever snare she's designed, but I want to see this goddamn carnival first.

"I'm not worried," she says. Darr grins like a mental deficient and Clay holds the front of the skiff flawlessly while we step out. He continues watching, searching—perhaps for the same answers I am.

"This what you were after?" he asks.

"I'm supposed to meet a geek here," I say.

"I thought you didn't know about the carnival."

"I didn't realize it was here tonight. "

"So why meet the geek?"

"He's got something important to tell me."

"How do you know that?"

"My best friend Drabs Bibbler mentioned it before the Holy Spirit took him away for good."

"I see."

Just saying it brings the rage kicking back into my guts. For the first time I believe Drabs' many tongues with true resolution. I hope he's here, if he's not already dead, so that I can beg his forgiveness for never doing a good enough job in defending him from God.

I know many of the folk as they wander by. I'm an anomaly here, but that's normal enough. I get smiles and offers of shine. There's Sap Duffy and Tab Ferris over there getting ready to draw knives over a fat woman whose thighs look like they might go on a rampage without her. Hert Plumb and Gussy Hocker are both chewing on fried frogs' legs that really belong to firebelly toads. Lonnie Dawson has a mouth full of jerky that's been cured for so long it might belong to the donkey that carried Jesus over the palm leaves.

It's not a carnival in any real sense of the word and hardly even qualifies as a festivity. This must be what it's like here when they're having one of their swamp weddings or revivals out in the bog. The folk are bored and restless but perhaps not as much so as usual. Almost none of them are daring enough to get onto the squealing, rusted rides. The clowns can only be picked out by their poorly painted features and shabby wigs. They wear the same clothes and boots as anybody else and they don't know how to juggle their little orange balls worth a shit.

Still, there is cotton candy and plenty of gator wrestling, ball throw and ring toss, and the occasional sprinkles of laughter. Small tents have been set up and are selling hot dogs, pretzels, and chicken wings. Trailers, trucks, and semi-cabs are lined up around the rides: they've got a five-horse merry-go-round, salt and pepper chug-a-lug shakers, the whirligig, and a small Ferris wheel that's maybe twice the height of a man. Darr was right. The gear boxes screech.

Somewhere nearby there's target shooting going on. Sounds like they're using 30-06 ammo, plugging anything crawling around on the embankments.

Darr finds himself some moonshine and offers it around. "Here, have a tap."

Lottie Mae is about to take a sip when I grab the mason jar from her and take a whiff. I pour a small amount of the shine into the metal lid. I flick my lighter and set the alcohol on fire, watching it burn. A solid orange flame flickers and pops.

"Dump it out," I tell him.

"Why? I just paid six bits for that."

"Good shine burns a low blue flame. This shit's been distilled through a car radiator."

Frowning, Darr takes a long swig and grins. "Nothing wrong with this. I've drank worse in prison. My pa used to make pruno out of raisins and rubbing alcohol, let it ferment in the toilet. He was a sterno drinker and I wound up with a taste for it too myself. Compared to that this shine is like two hundred year old brandy. Besides, it's a party. You're supposed to get fucked up."

We walk along for a while and I buy Lottie Mae some cotton candy. She's compelled to take it even though she doesn't seem to want it, or else she just doesn't want it from me. There's an odd but prevalent sense that we're on a chaperoned date that adds another element to everything we say and do. I almost enjoy it in a way.

After playing some ring toss and knocking down a few milk jugs with softballs, we wander around for another few minutes while I search for my brothers, Drabs, and the geek.

"Where's the sideshow?" I ask.

"Doesn't look like they have one," Clay says.

If they call this a carnival then there has to be a freak show, and the Holy Spirit has never lied to Drabs before. I keep my eyes open and so does Clay. Darr is getting pretty stewed and he's eaten five hot dogs already. He's got to heave pretty soon, I think, and I wonder what Clay will read in the vomit.

I spot a kid who's maybe ten years old, laughing his little ass off and carrying a water snake by the tail. It's a bizarre, ugly sound and it catches my attention. The boy slips through some mimosa leaves and heads behind one of the trailers. I follow.

"Where are you going?" Lottie Mae asks.

There's a crowd back there forming a circle. Sap Duffy and Tab Ferris are still pissed off about the fat woman, but they're interested enough to put it on hold for awhile.

I press my way through.

The geek rests in a mud hole surrounded by filthy straw while folks pitch pennies and toss snakes at him. Dogs snap and bark at him. He's lost both legs just above the knee and his left arm is gone at the shoulder. His beard is tangled with briars and there are open sores on his neck where he's rubbed himself raw in the sewage of the bayou.

He sucks at a jug of shine that wouldn't just burn a bright orange if you lit it, that booze would simply detonate. It's probably three-quarters radiator fluid.

Snakes land in his lap and he bites their heads off without fanfare. It means no more to him than chomping into a hamburger. No one in the audience gasps or claps or cares much at all. Half of them have handled serpents in church, and they've been bitten or done the biting many times before. This isn't freakish or overly-entertaining, but at least it's something to do.

Darr says, "Toss him two bits. I remember this guy from last year. He'll chew the head off anything. I'm not even sure if he takes all the money. Just enough to keep him in booze and he leaves the rest in the dirt."

"Leave me with him." My voice isn't entirely mine. It comes from far away and is brimming with subdued insanity. It whisks by and keeps on going.

"Pardon me?"

"You heard."

Darr isn't used to shine and it's made him a touch more belligerent. Violence wavers in his eyes. Maybe he wishes we had swords or sabers to duel with, just for the fun of it.

"I don't believe I liked the way you said that."

"I don't believe I care much."

"Uh huh."

"Go away."

Lottie Mae knows me well enough by now to begin plucking at Darr's arm, trying to draw him away. The seductive sex kitten is gone and I'm glad for it, I like her a lot better without the act. Clay cocks his head, curious about these unfolding events, wondering how they fit together and how they'll play out. Darr grins like he's got chicken bones jammed in his teeth.

I wait for it and it doesn't take him long. He throws a looping roundhouse right that's on target but way too slow. He hates fencing, he says, but really that's all we've been doing since we've met. I duck under his shot and keep going, dipping low until I'm at his boot. I draw the knife and hit the button, listening to the nice heady click of the blade popping open. I slash him in exactly the same place as before, right at the beginning of his middle strip of hair. Blood pours into his eyes and he roars with laughter. He trembles and his stomach rumbles and Lottie Mae and Clay drag him off into the brush where he throws up all his hot dogs and beer and shine. He doesn't want a fight, just some action. I know the feeling.

The geek looks up.

"Hello, Dad," I whisper.

HIS failures led him into the heart of the mill, where

he'd even failed to kill himself.

He doesn't recognize me. He lives inside his own etherized brain now. I spin in the silt and slime frothing beneath him as I get down on one knee and search his eyes, hoping to find some hint of the man he'd once been. There isn't any.

Folks are still tossing coins, vipers, chicken innards and dog shit. I pick up a cottonmouth snake, bite a chunk out of its tail and spit it back at them. It does the job and gets their attention.

I say, "That's enough for now. Get away from here."

Reactions range from melancholy to animosity, and I wait for somebody else to try something. They've all seen what's gone on between me and Darr, and I'm surprised to find that I'm still holding onto the switchblade. Faces begin to turn away. Sap Duffy and Tab Ferris get back to clobbering each other over the fat woman's unsightly thighs again. The kids start in on their cotton candy. A few of them collect the pennies left in the mud. There's no reason to waste good money if the geek's not going to eat shit.

Starving dogs nose at him, licking up the chicken parts. I shove them aside but they snarl and get right back on him until I grab a stick and start prodding them away. I notice that their rumps are covered with boot prints.

My father is unrecognizable but I still get the feeling they knew who he was and were just enjoying the hell out of the fact. I scan the area and know that Maggie's nearby. She's been with him since that day he leaped into the machinery of the mill, and she's taken care of him as best as she could.

What kind of luck, determination, will, or love has

saved him? He must've dragged himself free or been pulled out from the twisting, grinding, shrieking cogs and belts only to achieve this self-made fate. Christ, he must be laughing down there, deep down in his basal ganglia.

I grab him by the collar, lift and shake him. I yank him close until we're nose to nose. He weighs nothing, and I know that if I toss him in the air he'll just float away.

"Wake up," I tell him. "Dad. It's me. It's Thomas."

My name—which is his name—sounds strange and foreign to me, as if it should not be said aloud in his presence. He doesn't stir but his hand reaches out for his bottle. He doesn't even know that he's no longer on the ground. I slap him, trying to get him to focus on me, but if there's any spark of my old man left in there it's already run for cover.

Driven wild by his human needs, his lust for Maggie and his own guilt, incapable of stopping himself even after my mother found out, he was still compelled by his jealousy when Mama started stepping out. He couldn't bear the realization that she had become another juke joint swamp rat whore because of him.

"Look at me, Dad."

There's no reason for me to kill him if he doesn't know it's me doing it.

My father had discovered me that day sleeping near the corpse of a strangled boy. Did he think I'd done it? He must've hidden Johnny Jonstone's body and later on come back to retrieve it. My God, but why put the kid up in the attic? Why not kick him into the river? Instead he'd wrapped Johnny in plastic and laid him the trunk where his forefathers had laid all of their secrets as well. Was he doing it to protect me or only to punish himself? And how many times had he gone up there over the years and stared at that dried out mummified boy?

And there, behind the palms, I see my Dad's boots jutting out, same as the night I was hit by lightning.

It's the dog kicker.

I part the leaves and Maggie stands there in my father's shoes, filled with her own frenzy. I, who am her husband before the eyes of heaven, didn't ever really want her. But my father did.

No wonder she kicks dogs. She not only protects me but also guards my Dad. She has become his legs now, driving off the hounds that lap at his neck, but her anger can't be contained by the bayou. Every dog in Potts County is an evil reminder of what he's become.

"Where are my brothers?" I ask her.

She smiles and begins to laugh as she moves, in spasms, directly into my arms. Before I can hold her to me, and let loose with all that I want and all that I hate, she prances backwards out of my father's boots and vanishes into the scrub.

My father raises his eyes. Drabs said he'd talk to me for the price of a pint of moonshine. I toss six bits at the stumps of his legs.

"So, what do you have to say?"

His failures, defeats and near-sightedness have driven him to this, as mine have also brought me here. He had no other choice, which means that his love, and mine too, added to the killing of him.

In some ways he's better off than I am. His tongue slithers between his broken black teeth and swollen blue lips. He opens his mouth and begins laughing weakly, and hearing that hideous sound is like listening to a choir of ill children.

I leave the geek there in the mud, dead and giggling.

CHAPTER THIRTEEN

L EAVES slap against the windows and the whip-poorwills are calling. The hot night pours across my chest and the sweat streams down my burns.

She's back again, doing wild and furious things to me. That fiery red hair blazes in the darkness but shows nothing of her face except more shadow. Moonlight stamps in as I whimper at least one of the words she needs to hear. "Defeat." It raises a chuckle from someplace inside of her, buried and so far below that it sounds as if it's coming from under the bed.

I turn my face and look over at my brothers' sheets, expecting them to have returned to the house. I can't see through the blackness, but there seems to be motion over there. The room is packed with ghosts. Her languid cries bring them out of the walls, struggling and waving. She jerks to the side as if listening to my brothers moaning in their sleep. That darkness which comprises her concealed chin angles towards their bed as if listening to what is no longer there.

There's murder in the air but I don't know who's going to fall or why. It's there though, the taste under my tongue. Maybe it's her skin or breath, her very being and essence. If she is death then there ought to be more to it, I think.

She licks my wounds and makes soothing noises and tries to hug me to her breast, but I lay back. She moves against my legs and feet, working between my toes, using her nails to write out her meanings, her significance. These are the sentences of obscurity and void as she drips her gravy over me. I'm still trying to make out the wildly cursive script with all those well-defined stretches. They are like bodies placed upon me. There is weight to the words. My name keeps coming up in her footnotes. The index swirls around my thighs (*Ibid., Ch. 3, vi*) (*Ibid., Ch. 5, iii*) (*Ibid., Ch. 9, 'On Being Efficient', Pt I*). She slows down and begins printing with an even hand. *Girls: they accuse Rasputin of kissing with heavy tongue 32:67.*

It sounds like something I'd want to read. Now, she begins to write in verse. It tickles and I keep breaking into giggles. She shushes me and her hands flutter over my lips. She smoothes my burns, runs her fingers through my short hair. I can tell she likes it.

Her stiff, cold tresses unravel across the bed like eviscerations that never seem to stop. I try to talk to her but nothing much comes out but more laughter. The invocations are potent but not nearly powerful enough. They never have been. Her promises are lies, her entreaties worthless. She's known this from the beginning but she never did give up. I try to pat her shoulder but hit nothing but air. Her face is coiled in utter darkness but that doesn't matter anymore. The names she calls on will find little of value here.

I whisper, "There're going to be some changes. I'm tired of this game. Leave and don't come back." I reach over and turn on the light and there's nobody there. The wall shouts at me.

I add all this to the tally of my defeats but I will not sway from the course. The burning breeze scratches over my chest and I light a cigarette. I stand at the window looking down at the black lawn. The tupelo and cotton-wood sway in the hot breeze but there's nobody murdered in the yard. I'm filled with a kind of sorrow and longing that I can't explain. Ants are crawling up my back. Per-haps the storm is coming again. Or my brothers are head-ing home. I feel both foolish and larger than myself, glanc-ing up at the tree line and seeing the dark houses of King-dom Come in the distance, silhouetted in the moon. I turn from the window and somebody shuts off the lamp.

They move, in spasms, inside shadows whirling upon one another as if dancing. That massive bald head re-flects a smidgen of moonlight and my vision bucks with splashes of red as if I've been shot.

"You all knew Mama was up there all these years and you never said anything," I growl. "Why?"

With three mouths, in one voice, Cole, who speaks with love, tells me, "You weren't ready to listen, Thomas."

"That's not true, damn it."

"It is."

I take a deep breath and try to stay focused. It's diffi-cult and I feel as if I'm washing out at the edges. "And now?"

"Now you've no choice. None of us do."

My voice is flat and singular, more whiny than deter-mined. "You had no right to hide this from me."

They wave about like Mama's velvet curtains, palms brushing up against my arms, my face.

"Come home," I plead. "I'm sorry for what's hap-pened between us. I'll make it up to you, if I can."

"You can't," Jonah says. There is still great anger and

sadness in the lilt of the voice he presses up from their three throats. "You won't, and you shouldn't have to. But don't be sorry. It's not entirely your fault."

"That's very forgiving of you," I say, and I mean it, too.

"The burden has never been yours alone. It's ours as well, as it should be. Have faith in us."

"I do," I say, and I'm startled to realize I'm not lying.

"We'll be back."

"When?"

"Soon."

"Where will you go?"

"That doesn't matter. You're safer now without us near, and we're better protected without you around."

Jonah recites his poetry of regret, while Cole talks of devotion and Sebastian places his hands around my shoulders with a gentle pressure, as if testing what it might be like to either hug or asphyxiate me. He does neither. Molten silver bears down on us, but I can only see a hint of them as they lean and lunge. They're in pain, I can tell. It isn't easy reaching me this way.

"Do you know about Dad? That he's still alive?"

Sebastian laughs, a rumble of three sets of lungs, and the noise grows wilder and more wicked until three throats are nearly howling and I have to cover my ears. But I can't block out the sound and my mind is about to come apart.

I'm still like that, standing naked before the window with my fists pressed to my temples, the sun streaming in, when I awaken.

THE phone is ringing. I expect the incessant buzzing of my brothers' dismay but instead I hear Lily's frantic voice, imploring, strange and barely discernible. "Oh Jethus, I need you. Heth's crazy! Heth's going to kiw me!"

Private Eye Nick Stiel takes the phone from her and speaks very softly into the receiver. All he says is, "That's right." Whatever sorrow he'd been holding back has busted through the dam. As Lily shrieks in the background he lets out a mild sob and hangs up.

The sky darkens. I bolt out to the truck and race across town. I get to her place in under five minutes. By the time I climb out of the driver's seat she's already dead. Blood runs down her bay window and there are clumps of blonde hair sticking to the glass. I rush in the front door and nearly trip over her body.

Stiel is sitting on the couch, licking Eve's all day sucker. I find it unsettling but in a heinous way it's also something of a relief. His fists are bloody and he's got a snub-nose .38 in his lap, but there's no stink of gunpowder in the air. He eyes me calmly and says nothing.

Lily is lying face down on the carpet and the rug has soaked up most of her blood. I turn her over and wind up hissing through my teeth when I see what he's done. Stiel worked on her for a while, really taking his time. He knows pressure points, weak spots, nerve clusters. I could barely understand her on the phone because he'd knocked out some of her teeth and her lips had already been pulped. He must've loved her a lot to be able to do this with such vehemence. Her nose has been crushed, eyes nothing more than red smears smudged down her shattered cheeks.

"And Eve?" I ask.

He gestures towards the bedroom. I step in and see that the three of them have been into some pretty funky shit lately. There are sex devices, bondage para-phernalia, leather paddles, chains, weird-looking chairs and swings set up all over the place. Latex, collars, and whips that even Abbott Earl and the penitents wouldn't go near. Lily and I used to fool around with toys on occasion but goddamn.

Eve is dead on the bed in the midst of it all, dressed up in a lace nightie with matching gloves very much like the pair Lottie Mae wore that night in Leadbetter's when she got drunk. Eve's mouth is stuffed with a ball gag and her hands and legs are bound with intri-cately knotted ropes.

I draw her camisole off her shoulders. She has very ripe and firm breasts, but she's no little kid. Maybe eighteen or nineteen. It's obvious now that I see her with makeup on, naked, with a thick muff. There's a huge black bruise on her left side. It looks like he struck her only once, hard enough to break her ribs and drive them into her heart.

I back out into the living room and sit at the far end of the couch. He's no longer licking the sucker. It's on the carpet at his feet and he's tapping his toe against it like he's resistant to lose all contact.

"What happened?" I ask.

He picks up the .38 and points it at me. "There are two corpses in this house. One of them is a woman you used to screw. Doesn't that mean anything to you?"

"Yes, it does."

"You're unbelievable."

It seems that the people who question me the most are the ones who've committed the most outlandish or atrocious acts. I have no idea what that means. "What did you find out about the girl?"

His weariness bleeds from him like a cut throat. "What makes you think I found out anything?"

"You said you'd be on the case until the end. This is it."

Stiel scowls as if he's about to chastise me some more, but even he finds that ludicrous. "She was a prostitute from Los Angeles. I'd tell you her name but there's no point now."

"How'd she wind up in Potts County?"

"She came to join the Holy Order as a nun, if you can believe that, but she made so much money along the way that she decided to keep tricking. She specialized in the kiddie trade."

"Why the act?"

"She'd worked a lot of the county already. Ask any of the men at your mill. She was a smart pro."

That makes sense, and I try not to let the stench in this house of death drive me from it before I discover what I've come here to learn. "Yeah, smart enough to stay out of jail. So she was never picked up. Lily told me that Burke printed her but there was no match."

"She didn't hook on the street in L.A. and none of her dates ever would've opened their mouths about her. Her clientele was very loyal."

"I can imagine."

The stain around Lily's destroyed face grows larger and the flies are getting in. "She was making her way up to you. Figured there'd be big money in it one way or another." His face crawls in on itself as if trying to skitter off his skull. "She heard you went in for little girls."

"Hm. Why was she out at the flat rock?"

"I don't know. Maybe she was just lost. Maybe it was a way to pique your interest. Everyone knows you have a thing with that place."

"Why didn't she talk?"

It's getting harder for him to talk. The realization of what he's done grows stronger by the minute and the weight of his crime is crushing him to dust right before my eyes. He's starting to pant. "She couldn't. She's a mute. It made her a success out in L.A. A guy could do anything he wanted to her and she would never talk back to him. Never complain or argue or make any sound at all."

"You said she muttered in her sleep."

"She was traumatized as a kid. Something to do with her father. She never spoke again after that—except in her dreams."

The crawling scads of flies become louder, so much like the angry buzzing of my brothers. "What did she say then, Stiel?"

"Oh my Christ, you don't want to know."

"And you knew all of this the night you tore up Leadbetter's."

"Some of it."

"So why didn't you tell me? Why not just send her packing?"

"I liked it too much by then." His admission crushes the rest of the air from his lungs and he has trouble catching his breath. He gasps and wheezes and a wail of anguish threads everything he says. "Don't you understand? I went to bed with her before I knew anything. Do you realize what that makes me?"

She's older than Dodi, and probably older than Lottie Mae too. He's tearing himself up for being what I am. "Stiel, listen to me—things are different down here. This is the deep South. There are laws that don't apply."

"You're an ugly, disgusting people."

"No worse than most I'd guess."

I mean it as an honest assessment but he takes it as an insult. He squeezes his eyes shut but it's even uglier in there and he's got to open them again to get away from his mind. "I save children, that's what I do. That's what I'm supposed to do. In my mind and soul, do you know what I've become? What they made me into? I can't be let out on the street. Not now. Not anymore."

"Stiel, don't—"

He raises the revolver to his mouth and pulls the trigger, blowing all the screaming ghosts and demons out from his scattered three pound brain.

THE tempest returns, as it must. Lightning shears through the malevolent clouds as the assault begins. The river is in another frenzy. Rain claws for me through my windshield, flowing like arterial spray. The wind is one long lament. My skin is on fire, as if the very atoms of my body are calling the lightning down for another strike. Flames run across the woods, flickering against the splashing run off. The flooded roads wrangle me towards one corner of town and I go without question.

I drive to Velma Coots' place and can hear her screaming voice over the thunder and thrashing rain as I draw up. Dodi is in there too, yelling, "No, Mama, no!"

"Do it, chile!"

"I won't!"

"Do as I say!"

My roofing job has finally started to cave in. Rain boils into the shack through the ruptured beams and shingles. The brass cauldron in the fireplace spits black venom against the heated brick.

Velma Coots lies straddled over the chopping block. All her fingers are gone and the stumps of her hands have been cauterized and poorly tied off with strips of yellowed sheets. The burned flesh of those nubs still smells like sizzling steak. Dodi stands there with dark circles under her eyes. She holds a long-handled ax poised over her mother's neck.

The swarming water washes over them. Velma Coots cries again, "Mine me! Do it, girl!"

"No!"

Dodi hurls the ax at my feet, rushes out to my truck, guns the engine and wheels away, leaving me alone with this crazy granny witch on a night when the dead are climbing out of our heads.

"You go on and finish it," Velma Coots tells me.

"Cut your head off?" I ask. "What purpose would that serve?"

"Only purpose there is! Somebody got to make the sacrifice. You ain't gonna pay your debts."

"Oh shut the hell up about that, lady. I've been evening the score on them pretty well the past few days."

"Not enough," she sneers.

I help her to her feet and move her off to a corner chair where the roof still gives some shelter. "I suppose it's too late for that vinegar stuff."

"A'yup."

"Where are my brothers?"

"Doin' their part."

"Which is?" I try to imagine their stunted, gnarled

bodies out on the highway hitchhiking, waving down strangers. Six thumbs hanging in the vicious wind pointing in every direction.

"Too late to worry about it."

I snort and try another route. "Did you give Lucretia Murteen an abortion?"

"That woman wanted a child more'n anybody I ever known."

"Who did it?"

"You ain't ever gonna find out."

"Jesus, I wish you hags would quit saying that."

"Life's got more questions than answers, boy."

It hits me low and I burst out laughing. "You granny witches. You're so laid back about killers but you'll put your own neck on the chopping block. The fuck's wrong with you people?"

"It coulda been anybody. Maybe that Abbott Earl done it. He could be lying about what he heard and saw, you ever think of that? Maybe one'a them other monks. They got men floatin' around that place from all over the country, with their minds that ain't right. Drugs and liquor, torturin' one another in the name'a God hisself. They beat themselves bloody for redemption and then spit in the Lord's eye. It just don't matter. You ain't ever gonna know."

"Yes I will."

I head out. It's a long walk back home in the slashing rain but the storm begins to lessen while I'm on my way.

Dodi drives past without slowing down and I think I see an odd movement in the back of the truck. A tri-fold darkness and blur of black motion waving. And beneath the sound of the storm of souls, fluttering in my basal ganglia, a laughter like the muted song

of a choir of ill children.
    When I get back to the house the rain has ended.
    Drabs is hanging from a willow branch.

CHAPTER FOURTEEN

THREE days after Drabs' funeral the Reverend Clem Bibbler presides over my marriage to Maggie. He's also the best man and has to stop several times in order to wipe away his tears and calm himself. His voice quavers but his smile is sincere. Abbott Earl offers up prayers and litanies at sixth hour during the wedding. Most of the town turns out for the church service and there are lavish gifts, cards and favors, along with hundreds of homemade dishes. Even Sheriff Burke shows up in a good mood wearing lizard skin boots and a white ten gallon hat. We hold the reception at the house and he gets drunk on some good red wine, hits on the fat woman that Sap Duffy and Tab Ferris were fighting over, and eventually winds up sleeping it off in the bathtub.

Fred and Sarah come in from New York. They're both clean and sober, and Sarah shows off her engagement ring. Fred's documentary on addiction has won some festival awards and he's got a lucrative cable deal now. I decide to fund another project for him— an independent crime drama about a pair of hit men running from the mob who dress in drag and join a

Atlantic City lounge act. Sarah's written the script, which I read to Maggie one night in bed. I think it lacks a third act and make some notes in the margins with a red pen. Sarah and I discuss revisions and Fred uses the money to bring in two established actors. One is an Academy Award nominee, which will help to get distributors interested. Sarah takes the female lead and manages to hold her own pretty well, from what little footage I've seen. When we talk, she never asks about Jonah so I never mention him either.

Clay, Lottie Mae and Darr come to visit often. They all enjoy my sponge cake too. The mood is genial with hints of distress bubbling up from beneath, but eventually a much more mellow atmosphere takes over. Clay is quite talented at carpentry and I pay him well to rebuild a few missing shutters and fix up some other areas of the house that have fallen into disrepair. Perhaps he just wants a peek at the crannies of the place, which is also fine with me. I still don't know why they were killing all the birds.

Darr has taken up fencing, and I practice with him in the back yard. He wears a mask, plenty of protective gear, and a rubber tip at the end of his sword. He's actually quite good. He's got a much longer reach than I do, but he's slower, so we're evenly matched. I stock just enough liquor in the house to keep him pleasantly buzzed most of the time.

Clay and Maggie exchange long glances and share something beyond my understanding. It's all right because we're all protected here. The tempests and the dead come and go as they're meant to do. They bring their pain and we bring ours and together we fight our way to the dawn.

I've put Velma Coots up in one of the free rooms.

We've been spending time with some of the best doctors and mechanical engineers in the country fitting her with prosthetics. She wanted the hooks and cables, but I made her go for the gloveless endoskeletal hands with self-skinning foam. They're much more realistic and even higher functioning.

She tells me that she hasn't heard from Dodi and has no idea of her whereabouts, but she's lying. It's understandable. I know my brothers and Dodi are still together, close by, probably out in the bog shanty town. They remain her charges and she fulfills her duty. One day, I'm certain, they'll return as promised. We'll share whatever burdens must be shared for the sake of Kingdom Come.

THE Crone has taken over my brothers' bedroom. We've re-plastered and painted it a nice summer yellow. I've bought her a new wardrobe and she now wears sun dresses, orthopedic hose and sweaters with big pockets where she hides bits of food. She listens to plenty of Liberace CDs and she's become fanatic about the DVD player. Already I've purchased an extensive library of movies for her to watch, and she spends hours in front of the home entertainment center listening to the commentary tracks and viewing the outtakes and deleted scenes. Delivery men arrive at all hours of the day with packages containing boxed sets of classic 50s sit-coms and widescreen versions of the John Wayne Limited Edition Collection.

The other granny witches visit quite often. Velma Coots has gotten good with her new hands and she can handle small objects with great dexterity. The conjure ladies used to spend afternoons brewing po-

tions and making oxtail soup, but now they've taken
to playing pinochle and mahjong. Velma Coots is so
good with the prosthesis that she can sail the cards
across the table like a Vegas blackjack dealer.

Lottie Mae occasionally joins them but most of the
time she merely sits quietly and lets the conversation
circle around her. Often she stares towards the bottoms as if she's watching something off in the distance. She stares and frowns before turning again to
the discussion, smiling blandly.

I try not to gaze at her with any great longing but
it's difficult. My heart juts into my ribs and a soft
sorrow runs through me until the world begins to draw
sideways and the wind brushes my collar back.

The burns fade and my eyebrows fill back in, but
my hair doesn't grow anymore. Every day I look as if
I've come fresh from the barber. I still go on retreat
to the holy order as much as I did before, but I scan
Abbott Earl's face wondering if he was the one who
got Lucretia Murteen pregnant and then balked at his
responsibilities. I bake the morning bread, ride the
donkey, and contemplate our efforts to discover the
will of God. Sister Lucretia's white eye-patch watches
me closely as I wander through the empty maternity
ward thinking of her and newborn babies.

The carnival packs up and leaves town, traveling a
few more miles upriver every week until it crosses the
state line. It'll be back next year and Maggie and I
will visit again with a wretched man whose disappoint-
ments murdered my mother and drove him into the
unstoppable wheels of his one grand monument to
Kingdom Come.

I'll beat the hungry dogs from him and chase the
bog folk off. I'll stare him in the eye and pay him the

six bits it costs for a pint of moonshine, and when his blue runny lips quiver and begin to part I'll leave him there in the slime once more.

There are still frayed ends that I return to again and again, questions that will not go away. I vow to find the killer of my grandmother no matter how long it takes me. I will know who pinned her to the roof of her school with a reap hook, and I'll learn what the words on the side of the building meant.

Maggie gets pregnant and a new excitement fills all of us. Darr goes out and buys a tiny fencing outfit. Clay begins to carve and assemble a bassinet made completely from white oak.

The boys at the mill bring me gifts and good wishes, but there's an added worry in their eyes. Paul the foreman tries to give voice to it but can't quite pull it off. He wants to ask me if I'm afraid my wife will give birth to a monstrous three-headed being that will wallow in darkness and hide in the swamp and—

I smile evenly and dock him for the five minutes he's late that day getting back from lunch. He walks around the floor in a wide-eyed panic the rest of the afternoon, screaming at the workers, keeping the line rolling as I look down from my office window.

I still wonder about who carried the torches and chased Betty Lynn through the tobacco fields, and if they're still out there. Perhaps they believed that she was actually pregnant with my baby. If that's the case, then they may return when Maggie begins to show.

We'll be prepared. We have numbers. I track down all of Drabs' children in the county. There are fourteen of them, more than I had thought. I take care of their mothers and set up accounts for their futures, and we invite them over to our home and watch them at play on the swing and along the slopes of the property. Reverend Bibbler's laughter booms on the breeze as he plays with his grandchildren and he's taken to wearing short-sleeved shirts and shorts. I've set up jungle gyms and see-saws and slides out in the yard. Clay builds the playground so it'll hold up in a storm.

My mother is dead but she continues to dream.

I witness her as a girl with blonde curls draped across the shoulders of her gingham dress as she tugs at the coat sleeve of her father. She removes all the rat traps. She forgives the shortcomings and hangs near the ceiling and drifts to the corners at dusk. Her hands are ivory and she brushes them softly against my cheek. She has an incandescence that will never die out.

Mama has shown me this: Maggie and I will walk side by side through a field, carrying an infant. Maggie'll be wearing a sun dress and bonnet and somehow we will find wheat and stand in it. The baby will give a toothless smile and hold out his chubby hands as if the whole world is a rare and precious thing for him to hold. My wife will glance at me, radiant with the autumn sun, her hair coiling out from beneath the bonnet and struck by the sunlight in such a way that her features are suddenly blazing, as natural and perfect as the season itself.

Secrets still chase me down the long dimly-lit corridors of my life. Perhaps Drabs paid my debt for me or perhaps my brothers forfeited him. These walls are filled with history and heartache. The ham is still in the house. I go to the attic and stare at the trunk which no longer has a key. There are dozens of other locked drawers, chests, chiffoniers, highboys, cabinets, and old luggage. I wonder what's in them and what else my father has hidden up here. And his fathers before him? Any keys I find around the house I add to one large ring. One day I'll try them all, but not just yet.

We are a family. This is blood. The home is huge and there's room for plenty of healthy children. Ghosts will forever put in appearances, as they should. Our illusions have muscle and meaning. The past returns at midnight, in the heart of our dreams, and the rains and the willows forever remind us of the sacrifices we've offered and those we have yet to make.